I0666185

THE NEW SHERLOCKIAN

A collection of scholarly musings,
poems, pastiche & speculations
about the Great Detective
by various hands, from
The Sherlockian journal
With new additional essays

Chosen and edited by Kelvin I. Jones

First edition published in 2022
© Copyright 2022 Kelvin Jones

The right of Kelvin Jones to be identified as the author of this work has been asserted by him in accordance with the Copyright, Designs and Patents Act 1998.

All rights reserved. No reproduction, copy or transmission of this publication may be made without express prior written permission. No paragraph of this publication may be reproduced, copied or transmitted except with express prior written permission or in accordance with the provisions of the Copyright Act 1956 (as amended). Any person who commits any unauthorised act in relation to this publication may be liable to criminal prosecution and civil claims for damage.

All characters appearing in this work are fictitious. Any resemblance to real persons, living or dead, is purely coincidental. The opinions expressed herein are those of the author and not of MX Publishing.

Paperback ISBN 978-1-80424-131-8
e Pub ISBN 978-1-80424-132-5
PDF ISBN 978-1-80424-133-2

Published by MX Publishing
335 Princess Park Manor, Royal Drive, London, N11 3GX
www.mxpublishing.co.uk

Cover design by Brian Belanger

ACKNOWLEDGEMENTS

The editor is, first of all, indebted to Mr. Samuel Gringras of MAGICO, for suggesting to me the idea of an additional British Sherlock Holmes journal, way back in the 1980s, when the publication, THE SHERLOCKIAN, first appeared. I'm equally indebted to the many contributors to this relatively short-lived journal, for the quality and scholarship of their contributions. I also warmly welcome the new contributors, whose work, I'm most happy to say, matches the original submissions for their style, content, and solid scholarship. The world of Sherlock Holmes and Conan Doyle, that inspired creator of the world's most famous fictional detective, has produced some fine writing in both fiction and non-fiction terms, the latter often being referred to as the 'writings about the writings'. Ours is a broad and diverse Church, and I hope that is remains ever so. It would indeed be appropriate if this volume might encourage, in the future, other writers and authors to contribute more articles like these.

PREFACE

Way back now, in the early 1980s, Sam Gringras of Magico Magazine asked me to consider editing a second British Sherlock Holmes journal, which he hoped would match in content and style the standard of work then appearing in the renowned UK Sherlock Holmes Journal, then, as even now, produced by The Sherlock Holmes Society of London.

I had my doubts whether it would truly succeed, but I was pleasantly surprised when, after a short interval, a clutch of highly reputable Sherlockian authors' stories and essays began landing regularly on my doormat.

Unlike the Sherlock Holmes Society of London, we decided to open our doors also to pastiches, for we had both noted, through that post-copyright Doylean decade, their growing popularity among Sherlock Holmes aficionados, not only in the USA and Canada but also in the UK.

In those now far off times of manual typewriters and primitive Amstrad computer systems, the new journal, overseen and proof read by the diligent Sherlockian scholar, Jack Tracy, took a while to edit, but the result, when done, was both critically well received and, in its appearance, pleasing to the eye; small, pocket-friendly, but containing a wide variety of ideas and, as my friend and intrepid Holmes editor, David Marcum would surely agree, featuring Holmes stories that followed faithfully the spirit and very specific style of Conan Doyle's own original detective stories..

Moreover, I made it clear to authors wishing to submit Holmesian pastiches, that, regarding story length, there would be no upper or lower limit – a position to which I shall always emphatically abide, since quality, not quantity, is for me the determining factor; as may be duly noted in this present volume.

THE SHERLOCKIAN only ceased publication because of a change in my personal circumstances, and not, I hasten to add, because of a lack of interest on my part, nor that of the original publisher, Sam Gringras, who himself remained convinced of its potential popularity and scholarly contribution, to the ever growing and global world of Sherlock Holmes fans.

Therefore, I was very happy to resume, once more, the mantle as editor of this diverse volume, and I would be most happy indeed if other fans of Mr. Sherlock Holmes find the varied contents of this collection, as I did, amusing, innovative, speculative, and broad-based in its compass.

I only wish to add this observation; when re-editing the present volume, I was unable, purely for reasons of space, and not necessarily on grounds of quality, to include ALL of the many, equally well-researched, fascinating articles and Sherlock Holmes pastiches from the original issues.

Therefore, I can only hope, that if this present volume of THE NEW SHERLOCKIAN finds favour among the Holmes *cognoscenti*, maybe a second volume could in time, appear once again, to grace the bookshelves of those loyal and intrepid Baker Street fans, who never seem to have enough of reading about the life, times and exploits of Mr. Sherlock Holmes, by those diligent and imaginative authors, who continue to entertain and delight them in their most nostalgic, 'inner chamber of the heart, where it is always 1895.' *

Kelvin I Jones.

Liskeard, Cornwall.

Devil's Foot Country. September 2022.

* Not my own words, but those quoted by the late Vincent Starret, Sherlockian and author of *The Private Life of Sherlock Holmes.*

CONTENTS

1. Poem. A Study in Friendship by Kelvin I. Jones.

2. Sherlock Holmes Gets His Own Peak by Michael Hardwick.

3. Whatever Happened to Baby Rucastle? by Ray Betzner.

4. A Sherlockian Treatment of The Mystery of The
    Dedication to Shakespeare's Sonnets by Robert F. Fleissner.

5. The Rhetoric of Sherlock Holmes by Walter Armstrong Jr.

6. The Sherlock Holmes Collection at Marylebone Library
    by Catherine Cooke

7. Holmes and Watson: A Poem by C. Martin.

8. The Observance of Trifles by Grant Healy

9. Uncommonplace Books by Kelvin I. Jones.

10. The Origin of The Baskerville Family in Devon by
    A. Godfrey Hunt.

11. Sherlock Holmes by Rail by Kelvin I Jones.

12. The Hound of The Baskervilles De-Mythologised?
    by Robert F. Fleissner.

13. The Cromer Hound by Kelvin I. Jones.

14. The Strange Case of The Solitary Husband
    by David Stuart Davies.

15. From Afghanistan To Newport Pagnell by Denis Smith.

16. Sherlock Holmes' Encounter with Poisons by
    Raymond J. McGowan.

17.   The Sudden Death of Cardinal Tosca by George Cleve Haynes.

18.   Some Irregular and Not Entirely Reverent Ruminations on The Baskerville Knighthoods by Kelvin I. Jones and Roger Johnson.

19.   The Consulting Detective and The Literary Agent: An Untold Tale by Barbara Rusch.

20.   Sherlock Holmes and The French Connection

21.   by Wendy Heyman – Marsaw.

21.   "Now Look Here, Captain Croker,' by Roger Johnson.

22   A Note on Nicotine by Kelvin I. Jones.

22.   The Lincoln Street Minister by David Marcum.

23.   V341, a poem by Kelvin I. Jones.

THE TANTALUS

One of the scarcest of ephemera is the Sherlockian journal. Over the past fifty years, scores of small productions (many of them excellent) have come and gone, leaving the collector to scour the catalogues of second-hand booksellers in vain. Even those august organs, the Sherlock Holmes Journal and The Baker Street Journal, have not been without their teething problems. There was a time when the former plopped onto my doormat four times a year, and when the latter did not share the fate of the Marie Celeste quite so often in its long and distinguished. history (a fate now happily rectified).

The hard core still remain: a good half dozen of them (mostly American and Canadian), displaying the fruits of pensive nights and laborious days, the work of devotees fond of tickling at those inconsistencies in the Canon which we fellow Sherlockians pounce upon so joyfully.

What room is there, for another competitor?

After taking up the mantle of editor, this question was thrown at me by some correspondents.

There are a few possible answers.

There is always a need for a British journal which provides scope for the so-called 'Higher Criticism.' The prestigious Sherlock Holmes Journal finds scope for only a limited number of the longer pieces by new and old commentators alike, and is now entirely commission oriented. 'The Sherlockian' was in its time in a position to act as an alternative channel (I baulk at the word "competitor"). Then there is the knotty problem of pastiches. There are many who are sceptical of creative imitation and who argue that the fake can never rival the original. (However, is that its intention?)

It is the opinion of your obsequious and ancient editor that the pastiche should, and *must* be encouraged, if only to raise the standards of such literary endeavour and let in new blood, as has been already proved with David Marcum's top rated anthologies. British writers have both the language and tradition to provide the authentic touch in this field. Apart from the now almost classical work of Denis Smith (sic), however, the Brits have been somewhat inconspicuous in the field until a decade or so ago.

Finally, this journal aimed to provide a focus for work well done. Catholicity and diversity of taste were pre-eminent requisites. Length was always given the respect it deserved.

The Sherlockian world has narrow boundaries. Within those boundaries, however, lies a diversity of creative and critical talent which this journal always, in the days of Mr Samuel Gringras, the original publisher, actively sought to encourage. Many of the names that appear between the covers of this compilation are now already familiar to devotees. Let us hope that some more unfamiliar names will come to grace our pages, ere long, should there be again a demand for such writing.

—Kelvin I. Jones. 2022.

A STUDY IN FRIENDSHIP

A poem dedicated to Arthur Conan Doyle, his immortal detective, Mr Sherlock Holmes of Baker Street, and his faithful amanuensis, Dr John H. Watson. A first draft version of this piece first appeared in 'A Study In Verses,' published in 1984, by Samuel Gringras' Magico Magazine.

It is still there now, that lofty chamber,
Bristling with test-tubes and Bunsen lamps,
Glimpsed down a corridor of whitewashed walls,
The room where a catalyst sparked a friendship.
A nut-brown doctor and the young detective,
Thrown together by a chance encounter,
One with health irretrievably ruined,
Alone in the noise and the dirt of London;
The other, a strange and brusque-voiced recluse,
His head stuffed full of eccentric knowledge.

They met next day to inspect their rooms,
A cheerful suite with two broad windows,
Gleaming with silver and polished veneers,
Kept by the matronly Mrs Hudson.

As weeks went by, the doctor observed him,
This thin-faced, hawk-nosed, sharp-eyed man.
For days on end he might lie on the sofa,
Wrapped in a torpor of narcotic dreams,
Or spend long hours on the London Streets,
Returning at night in some odd disguise.

And so, as Watson had cause to remember,
On the 4th of March, on a fog-stained day,
When the dun-coloured streets threw shadows of hansoms
Across the wet panes of those hallowed rooms,

A sergeant of Marines, bearing a note,
Summoned them both to the Brixton Road.

So was begun the immortal friendship.
Fused by the drama of Lauriston gardens.
Sown were the seeds of a lifelong saga,
A partnership bound by a tangled skein.

Would we have been in those pipe drenched chambers,
Where the Morstan strong box yielded no loot,
That coal lit room with its curious strangers,
Where dire deeds were told of and of the Devil's Foot
Were inscribed with pride in the good doctor's hand,
That brave survivor of The Battle of Maiwand,
We too would have stirred to the call of danger:
'Come, Watson, come! The game is afoot!"

-        Kelvin I. Jones, September, 2022

SHERLOCK HOLMES ON THE SCREEN

By Roger Johnson

A good deal of information has become much more easily accessible in the past thirty-five years. I have not attempted to bring this article up to date by covering film and television since the mid-1980s, but I have, with the editor's agreement, added a few corrections and noted one or two revised opinions in an afterword.

I was recently told that the historical character who has been portrayed most often in films is the Emperor Napoleon. For myself, I rather doubt it. My money is on Sherlock Holmes. I make his total 142 at present, and I have certainly missed a few.

Holmes — without Watson — made his moving picture debut as early as 1900. The choice of words is deliberate, as Sherlock Holmes Baffled was not actually a film. It was made by Edison's American Mutoscope and Biograph Company as a series of prints for viewing in those machines that you used to find on seaside piers, where you looked through a slot and turned a handle to flick the pictures on and give the illusion of movement. That is was printed on cards and not on perishable film may account for the remarkable fact that this very first recorded performance of the Master has survived to the present day — though you can now see it, if you are lucky, from the comfort of a cinema seat. To be frank, though, its survival is about the only interesting thing about it. It lasts for less than a minute and shows a burglar entering Holmes's apartment and robbing it before the detective's astonished eyes, vanishing by means of primitive stop-motion trick photography every time Holmes goes to seize him, and finally disappearing altogether. *Voila tout!*

Other films -- all silent, of course, and mostly lasting no more than twenty minutes followed in pretty short order, though nearly all of them are long since lost. In 1905, the first named actor to play Holmes, Maurice Costello, appeared in the American Sherlock Holmes; or Held for Ransom. His was followed three years later by another American short, Sherlock

Holmes and the Great Murder Mystery, and a rare Italian entry, Rival Sherlock Holmes. Then the initiative passed to Northern Europe.

In 1908, the Danish company Nordisk began a series of thirteen shorts featuring various actors as the great detective — notably Viggo Larsen, Forrest Holger-Madsen, and Alwin Neuss. Like most of these early silents, the Nordisk films pitted Holmes against such popular but quite uncanonical villains as A. J. Raffles and Arsène Lupin. In all, they bore little resemblance to the real thing, and would not be worth spending much time on but for the fact that a handful of them have recently been found and restored to viewable condition. Nordisk did not have it all their own way, though, even in Northern Europe. When not acting for them, Viggo Larsen for one would be found playing Holmes for other companies in Denmark and Germany.

It was left to the English and the French to produce an approximation of the authentic Sherlock Holmes for the screen. Starting with The Speckled Band, the Éclair company made eight films during 1912 and 1913, all directed by the Frenchman Georges Tréville, who also played Holmes. All were based on Conan Doyle's original stories, and the author himself was involved to some extent on the production side. The films are now lost, but surviving stills show Tréville as a distinctly Gallic Holmes — wearing the sort of oversized cloth cap that we now associate with When the Boat Comes In and with a Gauloise drooping from his mouth.

The next actor worth noting was the first to be instantly recognizable as Sherlock Holmes — and, curiously enough, he was not an actor at all. James Braginton, gaunt, aquiline, and hawk-eyed, worked in the office of the British producer G. B. Samuelson and was spotted there by the director of A Study in Scarlet, George Pearson. The film seems to have been remarkably faithful to its original, with the singular exception that nowhere in it does Dr. Watson appear. A couple of years later, Samuelson produced another close adaptation, The Valley of Fear, but this time without Braginton, who had had his moment of glory. The new Holmes was H. A. Saintsbury, who was by no means new to the part. He had played it many times on stage, both in Conan Doyle's play The Speckled Band and in William Gillette's classic melodrama Sherlock Holmes.

Which brings us neatly to Gillette himself. In 1916, he finally committed his own performance as Holmes to film. It was seventeen years since he had first played the part on stage, and one reviewer remarked: "William Gillette as Sherlock Holmes, in moving pictures, even at the ripe age of 63 years, was a consummation devoutly to be wished." It makes the mouth water, but — alas — Gillette's Sherlock Holmes is yet another lost film. In England, meanwhile, we find something that does survive, and deservedly so. It is a singular phenomenon.

In a little less than three years, Eille Norwood played Sherlock Holmes in an astonishing total of 45 short and two feature-length films for the Stoll Picture Company. Norwood was much of an age with Gillette, and, just as Gillette was Sherlock Holmes to a generation of playgoers, so Norwood was to a generation of viewers. He did not actually look very much like Holmes, but somehow, he made himself seem the part. Conan Doyle said: "He has that rare quality which can only be described as glamour, which compels you to watch an actor eagerly even when he is doing nothing. He has a brooding eye which excites expectation, and he has a quite unrivalled power of disguise." In fact, if anyone other than Lon Chaney deserved the title "The Man of a Thousand Faces," it was Eille Norwood.

Hubert Willis, his Watson, was the first of note in the movies — but he was hardly "our" Watson. He was quite as old as Norwood, and appeared throughout white-haired and cleanshaven, playing the part as a sort of affable lapdog, an amiable duffer. The true Watson was to come, but not for many years yet.

It is worth noting here that the Norwood films, like all Holmes movies up until 1939, were set in what was then the present day. True, Conan Doyle's short stories were still appearing occasionally in The Strand Magazine, but he was careful to give them the setting of the 1880s and 1890s. If a Holmes film were made in 1923, you could bet that it would be set in

1923. An analogy is the consistent updating of the James Bond films from their true period in the 1950s and '60s.

The last notable silent film was made in 1922 by a major Hollywood studio, Goldwyn Pictures — but it was made in England, with extensive location work. In this new version of Gillette's play, Holmes was played by a younger and much better-known actor than Eille Norwood: the Great Profile himself, John Barrymore. His Watson was Roland Young in his first major part, and Barrymore later remarked that "that quiet agreeable bastard had stolen every damned scene." And Professor Moriarty was played by Gustav von Seyffertitz as a man both morally and physically corrupt. Barrymore clearly had great fun at one stage, when his Holmes disguised himself as this criminal grotesque. Until recently, this version of Sherlock Holmes was another lost film, but painstaking work by Kevin Brownlow and the original director, Albert Parker, has produced a truncated but coherent version reconstructed from various fragments. Some lucky Americans have seen it, but the owners, the Kodak Eastman company, seem sadly unwilling to let it leave the United States.

And so we come to talking pictures, and the All-Talking, All-Deducing Sherlock Holmes of Clive Brook, already established as "Hollywood's Perfect Englishman," who first played the great detective in an American film called The Return of Sherlock Holmes — though it is never made clear quite where he has been. Needless to say, the film bears little relationship to the book of the same name. Holmes, who looks far too young to have retired in the first place, is called out of retirement to help the grown-up daughter (!) of his old friend Watson. Watson is played as an elderly bumbler by one H. Reeves Smith, in contrast to Brook's rather priggish and supercilious Holmes. The action occurs mostly on an ocean liner, and of course Professor Moriarty is involved. One of the more interesting points of the film is that the actor playing the Napoleon of Crime is one Harry T. Morey — and if his name appeared in a telephone directory, it would read "Morey, Harry T.," which is a fair approximation of the way some people pronounce the Professor's name.

Brook played Holmes again four years later, for Fox this time instead of Paramount. The new film was called just Sherlock Holmes and was allegedly based on the Gillette play, though there is little evidence of this beyond the noncanonical romance between Holmes and Miss Alice Faulkner. What we get is Holmes updated with a vengeance, to the extent of inventing a ludicrous super scientific device for stopping a criminal's getaway car by projecting an Invisible Ray. There is a new Watson, a younger silly ass this time, played by Reginald Owen, but most of Holmes's confidences are shared with Billy the page-boy, an insufferable little brat portrayed by an American youth whose attempts at Cockney result in an "Ow blawmay, Guvnarr" accent. To compensate, there is a quite magnificently menacing Moriarty from the Scottish actor Ernest Torrence, wonderful in the early scenes at his trial for murder. Condemned to death, he quietly and sarcastically thanks the judge and prophesies that all those responsible for his predicament will precede him in death.

Also rather grotesquely updated is a British film of 1931, based closely on Conan Doyle's own play The Speckled Band. Holmes, played by Raymond Massey in his first screen role, has an office full of secretaries, filing cabinets, typewriters, and even a primitive computer. But, once those are out of the way, we are plunged into an atmospheric version of one of the best of the short stories. It is difficult to think of Raymond Massey as Sherlock Holmes (Dr. Gillespie, yes, or Abraham Lincoln...), but he turns in a sensitive performance, active or brooding as the occasion demands. And he is matched with one of the best villains going, Lyn Harding as Dr. Grimesby Rylott (sic). Harding had played the part many times on stage, and it suited admirably his rather old-fashioned, barnstorming style.

Two more single films from this period deserve notice. The year 1932 saw a British version of The Hound of the Baskervilles, the Holmes of which was played by a chunky actor named Robert Rendell. His high, intellectual brow suggested the great detective, though nothing else about him did. The script was written by Edgar Wallace, who seems to have turned in a competent but pedestrian job; it is hard to be sure, because the only surviving print of this film has lost its soundtrack. We can be sure, though, of A Study in Scarlet, made by a small American company a year later, as it survives intact. Despite the title, the story is quite new, a clever variant on the Ten Little Indians theme, but owing nothing to Agatha Christie, as it predates her famous novel by several years. It is a well-made and jolly film, lasting just over the hour, but its most remarkable feature is that Holmes is played by Reginald Owen, last seen as Watson to Clive Brook's Holmes! Owen does not look the part, but he is a good enough actor and sufficient of a Holmes fan for that not to matter. He was even responsible for writing the film's dialogue, and a very neat job he made of it.

Still, we could be forgiven for wondering where the real Sherlock Holmes had been all this time. Many people would argue that he had been at Twickenham Studios since 1931, in the person of Arthur Wontner. Here at last was the Holmes that Sidney Paget drew — tall, thin, hawk-faced, he was like a Strand illustration come to life. Well, almost. Wontner was no youngster, and his was a Holmes of retirement age, showing little trace of the man who had fought three rounds with McMurdo at Alison's Rooms and who could straighten a twisted poker with his bare hands. A gentlemanly and rather avuncular Holmes, this — but then, even Vincent Starrett thought that such "sentimentalising" of the character was essential. Wontner made four films for Twickenham. The first two — The Sleeping Cardinal and The Missing Rembrandt — were much closer to the real thing than any since Eille Norwood's time, and the fourth was a good try at Silver Blaze. But the third was a classic.

The Triumph of Sherlock Holmes is based pretty solidly on The Valley of Fear, though the writers, with some justification, have added Professor Moriarty as an active character. And such a Moriarty! A melodramatic heavy of the old school, quite unlike Conan Doyle's subtly sinister criminal genius, but hamming it up gorgeously. Yes, it is our old friend Lyn Harding again. It must be said though, that the updating of the story to contemporary times does rather grate, especially in the American sequence, where the miners and Scowrers of Vermissa Valley look rather like a bunch of lounge-lizards dressed up for a tramps' supper. Still, it is a brave try, and far ahead of most of its predecessors.

Dr. Watson in these films is played by an actor called Ian Fleming, who appears as a prissy, self-important little man, very dapper, with iron-grey hair and a neat moustache. He is an improvement on Hubert Willis but might have been better cast as Hercule Poirot's friend Captain Hastings. There was a fifth film, though, in which Fleming did not appear. In the middle of the Twickenham series, another company, Associated Radio Pictures, employed Arthur Wontner to play Holmes in a version of The Sign of Four, directed with great vigour by the American Rowland V. Lee. Wontner wears an obvious hairpiece — which still manages to make him look ten years younger and the whole thing is much less sedate than the Twickenham films. In this story, of course, Watson woos and wins the lovely Mary Morstan, so a younger actor than Ian Fleming is required. And, in fact, Ian Hunter, who played the part, was only 29 years old.

Meanwhile, there was a younger actor than Arthur Wontner waiting to play Sherlock Holmes, and one who looked just as authentic. Basil Rathbone, of course. Twentieth Century — Fox went all out to make their production of The Hound of the Baskervilles a classic, and they succeeded superbly. Here at last, Holmes was not only the dreamer and the thinker but the man of action. And here at last was a company who realized that the detective belonged truly to the decades at the end of the nineteenth century. Sets, costumes, script, direction, and casting were all first-rate. And yet — we still did not get the true Dr. Watson. Nigel Bruce's interpretation is still, and rightly, remembered with great affection — but it is hard to imagine this dear old duffer writing those magnificent accounts for The Strand Magazine. It was not too bad in this first film, or in the second, but after that...

Ah, that second film! The Adventures of Sherlock Holmes had a completely new story, but if anything was better than its predecessor. Cunning, suspenseful, atmospheric — and above all, tremendous fun, particularly in the delicious verbal sparring between Holmes and one of the best Moriartys ever, George Zucco. This was perhaps Zucco's best part, and he made the most of it. But then things began to deteriorate. Fox did not want to be committed to a series, so Universal took over — and the first thing they did was abandon the faithful nineteenth-century setting. There were twelve films in the Universal series. Some (Sherlock Holmes Faces Death, The Spider Woman, The Pearl of Death) were pretty good; some (Sherlock Holmes in Washington, Pursuit To Algiers) were pretty awful; most were just average programme-fillers. But all were worth watching, because of Basil Rathbone. Yes, and because of Nigel Bruce, though by now he fitted perfectly the description "Boobus Britannicus."

Meanwhile, there had been one or two individual television adaptations made in America, but the first Sherlock Holmes series was that produced by the BBC in 1951, with Alan Wheatley and Raymond Francis as Holmes and Watson and scripts by C. A. Lejeune. It seems to have been a worthy effort (it was reviewed favourably in The Times), but there is no way to tell now, as of course all television was live in those days. There were no recordings. Stills suggest that Wheatley and Francis were well enough suited to their parts, and the designers seem to have done their job admirably. Less successful was a film series started in the same year. In fact, it was so unsuccessful that only the first instalment, a version of The Man with the Twisted Lip, was ever made. The general view seems to have been that it was thoroughly turgid. For the record, Holmes and Watson were played by John Longden and Campbell Singer.

But both these efforts are thoroughly overshadowed by the success of a series of no fewer than 39 half-hour films which are still being shown on American television today. They were made in France by the American producer Sheldon Reynolds, and, though most of the stories were apocryphal, on the whole they were pretty neat. Sets and costumes were good, and the largely British cast did their job very well. They were led by Ronald Howard as a competent if rather lightweight Holmes, Howard Marion Crawford as a first-rate, solid, no-nonsense Watson, and Archie Duncan as an unexpectedly bulky and Scottish Inspector Lestrade. In recent years, Sheldon Reynolds has gone back — this time to Poland — to see what more the mine will yield. His new Holmes and Watson are Geoffrey Whitehead and Donald Pickering, while Lestrade is played by Patrick Newell.

Colour enters the screen history of Sherlock Holmes as late as 1959, in the Hammer version of that old favourite The Hound of the Baskervilles. It is an uneven production, largely because the scriptwriter took too many liberties with the plot. Some of his changes work (Miles Malleson playing Frankland as a delightfully dotty old Bishop), but more do not (webbed hands, forsooth!). And what of the leading actors? André Morell is perhaps the best Watson to date — in fact, one of the best ever: stalwart, loyal, and intelligent. This is the man who wrote for The Strand Magazine. Peter Cushing gives a meticulously careful performance, but, as the critic of The Times observed, the affectations are just a little too affected. All might have been well, even so, but for one strange quirk of casting. Peter Cushing is six feet tall (which, according to Holmes in both "The Three Students" and "The Abbey Grange", is precisely right), but he is flanked by two of the tallest men in British films, Christopher Lee and Francis De Wolff, who at six feet four inches tower above him.

Some critics had noticed the tall, thin figure of Christopher Lee as Sir Henry Baskerville and wondered why he was not playing Sherlock Holmes. A few years later, that was rectified, after a fashion, in a German/ Italian/ British/ French co-production called Sherlock Holmes and the Deadly Necklace. The idea was for each of the cast to speak in his or her own language — then, for release in, say, Britain, the French, German, and Italian would be dubbed into English while the voices of Lee and Thorley Walters (as Holmes and Watson) remained intact. But it seems that the original soundtrack was lost, and, instead of the original cast, passing pedestrians were called in for the dubbing. It certainly seems likely, but in any case it was a curious production. The script by Curt Siodmak was tortuous, the direction by Terence Fisher pedestrian, and the designers apparently unsure of the difference between 1890s London and 1920s Vienna.

Better was to come in 1965, with a new Holmes and Watson in A Study in Terror. John Neville does not look quite right as Holmes (perhaps it is his hairstyle), and Donald Houston's Watson is just a little too eagerly amazed at his friend's deductions, but they are eminently acceptable in this clever original story which pits Holmes against that archetype of Victorian murder, Jack the Ripper. The casting throughout is quite outstanding; in particular, Robert Morley as Mycroft Holmes and Frank Finlay as Inspector Lestrade give what must surely be definitive performances.

In this year, too, the BBC made a new series. A version of The Speckled Band, included in a series called Detective, had proved successful enough for the same Holmes and Watson to be brought together again with some fine supporting actors, good scripts, and competent directors. The series was recorded, but sadly, no longer exists, though many of us recall it with great fondness. Some of the stories suffered a little from being stretched to fill a fifty-minute format, but the general standard was very high. Douglas Wilmer and Nigel Stock were admirable as the detective and the doctor, and there were particularly fine performances from Peter Madden as Lestrade and Derek Francis as a Mycroft to rival Robert Morley's in an excellent adaptation of The Bruce-Partington Plans.

Douglas Wilmer turned down the series that followed in 1968, because he thought that the schedule was far too tight, so Peter Cushing was engaged, and we are presented with a rather older Holmes and Watson. Nigel Stock still plays the good doctor, but tailors his performance to Cushing s. Wilmer proves to be right, and the resulting series is very variable. Some instalments, such as The Naval Treaty, are very good, but others are pretty awful. William Lucas is a competent Lestrade, but Ronald Adam is utterly miscast as Mycroft in a poor adaptation of The Greek Interpreter. His elderly, bald, wrinkled, friendly bloodhound face makes him look like everybody's favourite great-uncle. Still, it is not all bad, and it would be nice to see it again.

In contrast, Billy Wilder lavished an extraordinary amount of time and money on his feature film The Private Life of Sherlock Holmes. The result was not a commercial success, but it is immensely entertaining, and it looks better each time one sees it. There are strong echoes of the original stories, but ultimately the film is sui generis. Part of the problem for the Sherlockian is that Robert Stephens and Colin Blakely are just not our Holmes and Watson. And as for casting Christopher Lee as Mycroft Holmes

. . . ! Yet, on its own terms, the film works. It is bizarre, outrageous, inventive — and ultimately charming — and perhaps this strange affair of the Belgian Engineer and the Loch Ness Monster does reveal something of the private life of Sherlock Holmes. At all events, it must be the most quotable of all the apocryphal adventures. "Big Dog from Baskerville" indeed!

Parodies abounded in the 1970s. John Cleese made a couple of rather surrealistic television films, Elementary, My Dear Watson and The Strange Case of the End of Civilisation As We Know It, which were very entertaining but contained a good deal more of John Cleese than of Sherlock Holmes. Peter Cook and Dudley Moore managed to ruin some of their own funniest jokes in a thoroughly contemptible send-up of The Hound of the Baskervilles, which deserves a dishonoured place on anyone's list of The World's Worst Movies.

Two parodies deserve some comment, though. James Goldman's 1972 film They Might Be Giants is not really about Holmes at all, but about a twentieth-century American who believes that he is Holmes. George C. Scott and Joanne Woodward are quite excellent as the madman and his reluctant psychiatrist — whose name, of course, is Dr. Watson. This charming film is perhaps too rarefied for most people's tastes. (The title derives from the lunatic's perceptive comment that Don Quixote was mad because he thought that all windmills were giants, while the wise man is aware of the possibility that they might be giants.) In 1975, Gene Wilder followed his success in Mel Brooks's Young Frankenstein with his own spoof The Adventure of Sherlock Holmes' Smarter Brother. The brother in question is not Mycroft but a hitherto unknown younger — and insanely jealous — sibling named Sigerson. Sherlock and Watson do appear, played by Douglas Wilmer and Thorley Walters, and generally are treated fairly straight. But Sigerson (Gene Wilder), his friend Orville Sacker (Marty Feldman), Professor Moriarty (Leo McKern as a sort of Irish Lyn Harding), and the rest of the crew are pretty outrageous. As a Sherlock Holmes film, it is a non-starter, but its energy and sheer youthful verve make it a highly entertaining comedy.

Universal, meanwhile, had trotted out the poor old Baskerville Hound in a version made especially for television, but the script was mediocre, the casting poor, and the design frankly bizarre. Once again the old Mittel European sets from the pre-war Frankenstein films were put to uses they were never intended for, so that one half-expected the Burgomeister of Coombe Tracey to appear on his balcony and urge the peasants to go out with their flaming torches and hunt down the monstrous hound. Bernard Fox simply bumbled as Watson, without showing any of Nigel Bruce's charm, and Steward Granger was just plain wrong as Sherlock Holmes — especially as most of the time he appeared to be dressed as a Mississippi gambler.

The next major feature film was much better. This was The Seven-Per-Cent Solution, written by Nicholas Meyer and based on his bestselling novel. In this ingenious story, Holmes's cocaine addiction has progressed so far that Watson has to lure him to Vienna — with the help of Mycroft Holmes and a reluctant Professor Moriarty, whose villainies exist entirely (or almost entirely) in the detective's drug-confused mind. In Vienna, he is to be treated with the radical new techniques of Dr. Sigmund Freud. Laurence Olivier's whining, cringing Moriarty is quite riveting, and Alan Arkin is excellent as the young Freud. But what of Holmes and Watson? Nicol Williamson, as one critic observed, is about as aquiline as a boiled potato; with his sad, hangdog expression, he is to Sherlock what Ronald Adam was to Mycroft — but his nervous mannerisms, his rapid deductions, and his impatience with lesser minds are all part of an excellently observed performance. Robert Duvall looks like Watson, and behaves like Watson, but he does not sound like Watson. He is not one of the few American actors who can assume a flawless English accent, and his curious if brave attempt grates throughout the film. But generally speaking it is a most entertaining romp, which still manages to treat seriously the serious matter of drug addiction.

Holmes's drug addiction was on Christopher Plummer's mind, too, when he first played the detective in a 1977 television adaptation of Silver Blaze. In fact, he was rather good, and he looked the part, being as aquiline as Nicol Williamson was not. His Watson was reliable old Thorley Walters, so all should have been well, but the flat direction and inadequate script disappointed. Somehow, the famous exchange about The Dog in the Night-Time was completely omitted.

At about the same time, a much less likely actor was playing Holmes in an American television film, and making a surprisingly good job of it. The star of Sherlock Holmes in New York was none other than Roger Moore, with Patrick Macnee as a disappointingly subdued Watson. Moore, though, positively bubbled. Disregarding the fact that he was too impossibly handsome to look like Holmes, he seized the part with both hands and made the most of his exchanges with John Huston's outrageously Irish Professor Moriarty. It all came about because Twentieth Century Fox thought it a pity to waste their beautiful 1890s New York set after the completion of Hello, Dolly! and had engaged Alvin Sapinsley to write an ingenious story about an impossible bullion robbery involving Holmes, Watson, Moriarty, and the woman, Irene Adler. The result was a highly enjoyable slice of hokum.

Murder By Decree, the next film to appear, was much more serious, even sombre, in tone. Christopher Plummer gives a mellower and more considered performance as Holmes, and his relationship with the excellent Watson of James Mason is a joy. The only adverse criticism would be that, at 68, Mason was nearly twice the age that Watson would have been in 1888. Yes, we are back with Jack the Ripper, but, unlike A Study in Terror, this film is based on a serious (if now discredited) theory about the identity of Saucy Jack. Perhaps this accounts for the occasional loose ends in the script. But quibbles aside, Murder By Decree is a compelling and highly atmospheric film, with fine performances from all concerned. It is a particular pleasure to welcome back Frank Finlay's definitive portrayal of Inspector Lestrade.

In 1982, the BBC decided to make a prestigious production of the most famous Sherlock Holmes story of all. It was meticulously planned and very faithfully adapted, proving that the changes made in previous versions really were not necessary. So why was not this Hound of the Baskervilles instantly hailed as a classic? The answer lies in the casting. To have Tom Baker play Sherlock Holmes when he had been so long identified with another legendary hero was a bold move but not a wise one. His acting is unexceptional; it is just that he is not Sherlock Holmes. He looks quite wrong. Terence Rigby, on the other hand, gives every evidence of having once been a champion rugger player, but his Watson is not so much a bumbler as a pudding, stolid and thoroughly dull. Any sort of relationship between this Holmes and this Watson must have been tedious in the extreme.

And the Americans were doing no better. Sy Weintraub had started well, by signing up that admirable actor Ian Richardson to play Holmes, and a good cast of British actors, for his production of The Sign of Four. There were Thorley Walters, Cherie Lunghi, Joe Melia and others — and David Healy as Dr. Watson. But it does not work. The production and script are frankly shoddy. Chunks of Billy Wilder's witty screenplay for The Private Life of Sherlock Holmes have been incorporated, but to little effect. Even so, there was a follow-up, but, despite good support from Martin Shaw, Denholm Elliott, Glynis Barber, and Brian Blessed, it was no better. Donald Churchill turned in a blimpish performance as Dr. Watson, and the whole thing put paid to the producers' hopes of a full series. It was all very sad, because in the right circumstances Ian Richardson could be one of the best Holmeses yet.

The British television companies, meanwhile, were concentrating with great success on a younger audience. The BBC's clever and charming little series The Baker Street Boys was not actually about Sherlock Holmes at all, but about his little band of street urchins, the Baker Street Irregulars. Holmes and Watson are glimpsed occasionally, but the Irregulars are definitely the main characters, applying successfully the methods taught to them by the Master. Granada Television offered a fine nine-part serial called Young Sherlock, which presents the adolescent Holmes a cunning opportunity to exercise his fledgling detective powers. The writer, Gerald Frow, clearly knows his Canon thoroughly, and Guy Henry as the young

Holmes is so strikingly good that I hope we may in time have the chance to see him play the adult Holmes.

But Granada had not concentrated solely on the youthful Holmes. Even while Young Sherlock was being shown, a lavish and accurate series was in preparation, based on Conan Doyle's original stories, and in 1984 it reached our screens. The supporting casts revive happy memories of the BBC plays of twenty years before, while the new Holmes and Watson are a revelation. David Burke is the authentic Dr. Watson, impetuous, intelligent, humorous, loyal, courageous — and sufficiently tolerant to bear with the moody eccentricities of Jeremy Brett's Holmes. And in Brett we find the true manic-depressive that we see in the pages of The Strand Magazine, the man who loathes every form of society with the whole of his Bohemian soul, the genius and the loner. The suspenseful scripts occasionally diverge from the original stories, but always with good reason. The direction is first-class. And the Holmes and Watson fit perfectly into the jigsaw: their appearance and behaviour are utterly right, and their relationship thoroughly believable. That first series of seven stories was a winner all round, and the second (shown in 1985) lived up to it, culminating as it did in a superb adaptation of The Final Problem. Eric Porter oscillates wonderfully in an electrifyingly sinister performance as Professor Moriarty, and location filming was never better used than in the fatal conflict at the Reichenbach Falls.

And there was a Christmas treat in 1984. A good story and a first-rate script had tempted Peter Cushing to take up the deerstalker and pipe again and portray the elderly Holmes foiling a devilish plot that prefigures the Great War. In The Masks of Death, everything went right: script direction, design, casting — and, among a distinguished cast, the performances of Cushing and John Mills as Sherlock Holmes and Dr. Watson stood out. Their companionable relationship was pure delight. At last, Cushing had found the perfect vehicle for his portrayal of the Great Detective.

And so we come to 1986, and in utter contrast to the elderly Holmes of The Masks of Death we have Nicholas Rowe as Young Sherlock Holmes. Do not expect the canonical fidelity of Gerald Frow's Young Sherlock: the

19

new film shows Holmes and Watson meeting as schoolboys. We know that they did not, but this is an admitted fantasy, providing great fun as it plays the game of "let's pretend." For me, Nicholas Rowe lacks something in comparison with Guy Henry, but he puts up a very good performance, while Alan Cox as Watson is even better. One can imagine this young Holmes and this young Watson growing up to become — well, if not Basil Rathbone and Nigel Bruce, then perhaps John Neville and Donald Houston.

And the game is still afoot. In Hollywood, the Walt Disney Studios are preparing a full-length cartoon based on Eve Titus's charming tales of Basil of Baker Street, a mouse who lives in the cellars of 221B and applies the Master's methods to cat and mouse crime. Peter Cushing and John Mills are together again, making a follow-up to The Masks of Death, to be called The Abbot's Cry. And perhaps the best news is that we can expect to see Jeremy Brett again in a new series of The Adventures of Sherlock Holmes, though without David Burke. The new Watson will be that fine actor Edward Hardwicke, and I have every hope that he will live up to the standard set by his predecessor.

Afterword

Maurice Costello was long credited as the first to play the great detective on film, but Howard Ostrom has convincingly identified the actor in the 1905 Sherlock Holmes, or Held for Ransom as Gilbert M. 'Broncho Billy' Anderson.

Despite my confident assertion in the article, publicity stills do clearly show Dr Watson among the characters in George Pearson's 1914 A Study in Scarlet, though the name of the actor, like the movie itself, is lost.

A good negative of the 1916 film Sherlock Holmes, based on William Gillette's play and starring Gillette himself, was discovered in Paris and a restored print has been released on DVD and Blu-Ray.

In Albert Parker's rather less faithful 1922 adaptation of the Gillette play, John Barrymore's Holmes does not in fact disguise himself as Professor Moriarty.

Peter Cushing actually stood two inches under six feet in his prime, but – like Sherlock Holmes – 'was so excessively lean that he seemed to be considerably taller'. Douglas Wilmer was the same height, but in both the 1965 and 1968 BBC TV series careful casting ensured that the actor playing Holmes was not made to look small.

The 1965 BBC series with Douglas Wilmer, and the previous year's production of The Speckled Band, survives almost complete, and the episodes have been restored by the British Film Institute and released on DVD. Of the 1968 series with Peter Cushing, only six episodes survive, and are available on DVD. Among them is the two-part Hound of the Baskervilles, which ranks with the 1939 Fox film as the best screen version of the story.

Possibly I've just got used to Robert Duvall's attempt at a British accent in The Seven-per-Cent Solution, but I do now think my criticism was unnecessarily harsh.

The 1977 Harlech Television production of Silver Blaze, starring Christopher Plummer, is actually far better than I remembered. At less than thirty minutes, there is no room for padding – but the famous exchange about The Dog in the Night Time is there, intact.

Having the chance to see the 1982 BBC TV Hound of the Baskervilles again, I have had to revise my opinion of his performance and of Terence Rigby's. The four-part production is well worth a look, if you can find a copy.

SHERLOCK HOLMES GETS A PEAK OF HIS OWN

By Michael Hardwick

Holmesians will need to look to their revisions. From October 5, 1984, that hitherto nameless feature which stands where 36° 12' 26" N and 96° 02' 56" W intersect, in the northeast quarter of the south west quarter of Section 17, Township 20 N, Range 12 E of the Indian Meridian in Osage County, Oklahoma, has been officially Holmes Peak. The United States Board on Geographic Names convened on that day and declared it so, and a Holmes Peak Preservation Society is already vigilant against any neglect.

The naming marked the culmination of a dogged struggle against legislative and ecclesiastical bureaucracy. A Tulsan gentleman, Dick Warner, who holds the office of Head Sherpa in that esoteric society named the Afghanistan Perceivers "You have been in Afghanistan, I perceive," remarked Sherlock Holmes upon first meeting Dr. John H. Watson), noted that, while the Moon had its Sherlock Crater, there was no place like Holmes on Earth. He found a candidate a mere two kilometres south-east of Tulsa's city limits. It seemed to have everything, elevation (314 metres above sea level), a certain unspoiled grandeur, historical associations of not too dogmatic a kind, and a rich variety of flora and fauna, the latter including reported sightings of the unicorn and yeti. What it did not possess was a name.

With a certain naiveté, Warner assumed that the U.S. Government would leap at the opportunity to demonstrate its respect for the Sage of Baker Street and preeminent private consulting detective. The Government did not leap. There had to be Procedures. Ownership of the land had to be established.

Elementary! The Osage Indians, whose reservation the territory had been declared in 1870.

It took two years for Warner to establish that, while there are Osages remaining and drawing oil royalties, the owner of the peak land itself had been dead since 1982, which was why he had not replied to letters. He had bequeathed his holding to the University of Tulsa, Oral Roberts University, and the Catholic diocese.

The two former persons made no objection to a submission to the Board on geographic names. The bishop of Tulsa, however, found the idea frivolous and vetoed it. Warner wrote to the Pope. In case His Holiness might have gone a trifle rusty on a particular aspect of hagiology, he was reminded that, in 1890, Sherlock Holmes had obliged a predecessor of his in a matter of some missing cameos. If he did not do so, Warner might well have pointed also to the common ground of papal infallibility and Holmes's conceit of himself as "last and highest court of appeal in detection."

Instead of a note of thanks and benediction, the Vatican's reply came in the form of a bull to the bishop of Tulsa, who, not unnaturally, protested at the matter having been carried above his head. At the same time some sixty natives, male, female, and juvenile, some dressed tropically and sporting insignia of the British Army and Royal Marines, pressed forward. Libations of a beer-like appearance and taste were proffered. I was conducted eagerly to an awning, under which assorted viands lay ready. Seating had been rudely improvised from bales of hay.

An ensemble of brass instruments played. Bagpipes droned and drums clamoured. Voices were upraised in a semblance of "God Save the Queen." It was almost unbearably moving.

Called on to speak, I gave some modest account of my scramblings on Vesuvius and Adel Crag, and disclosed my ambitions toward Mount Washington, Pittsburgh. After awed acclamation, I was borne summitwards in a pick-up; had I had to climb, vertigo and altitude sickness must surely have claimed me.

As to the view from the summit, there are really no words. The Japanese say there are two kinds of fool: those who have never stood on top of Fujiyama and those who have done it more than once. That is just about it, in a nutshell.

What shall I say of Holmes Peak itself? Elemental? The treelessness under that burning sun, the coarse shrub, the rubble! Primeval? Warner has identified fossil fragments as crinoid, bryzoans, and molluscs, together with such sedimentary traces as drag, gouge, and flute casts, from which he, correctly, adduces deltaic orgins.

The ceremonies ended with a firework display and the flying of flags on the peak against a golden sunset. Camp was struck. The bunting was taken down and the haybales lifted. The marker we had unveiled was removed, I the certainty that, if left there, it would get shot up inside 24 hours.

Fantasy? I prefer the allied word, myth: an extension of one of man's most pervasive mythologies.

Through such enterprises as the naming of Holmes Peak, myth, legend, and human comradeship are refreshed and nourished. For a few hours in Oklahoma, it seemed that George. III and Lord North had never existed.

This article originally appeared in the Washington Post in January 1986 and is reproduced by permission of the author.

WHATEVER HAPPENED TO BABY RUCASTLE?

A Tale of Canonical Lycanthropy

Ray Betzner

In his final paragraph to the adventure of The Copper Beeches, Dr, Watson gives us what television newscasters would call an update. Watson's little epilogue mentions each of the characters from the adventure and presents us with his history after leaving the realm of Holmes's interest.

One person is missing from the epilogue - Edward Rucastle. Why, l wondered, should Watson go through all the trouble of tracking down the lives of the others and leave out the most remarkable of the story's characters? In short, what happened to Edward Rucastle? His father, Jephro_ believed we would all know the answer to that question. The senior Rucastle boasted that his son "may someday play a considerable part in the history of the country." But Jephro Rucastle's hopes for a famous son, like his plans against his daughter, failed. Edward's name is absent from the major histories of Great Britain and is not to be found in such works as The Dictionary of National Biography, Who's Who or The Name Index in The Times.

Having failed to find Edward outside the Canon, l resumed my research by going back to the events recorded by Watson.

We know that Edward is the younger, hence the baby, of the two children fathered by Jephro. Edward is also the only child from Jephro's marriage to the morose second Mrs, Rucastle. Jephro described the boy as "one dear little romper, just six years old. Oh, if you could see him killing cockroaches with a slipper. Smack, smack, smack! Three gone before you could wink! "

Miss Hunter's description is even more disturbing. Edward is "small for his age, with a head which is quite disproportionately large. His whole life appears to be spent in an alternation between savage fits of passion and gloomy intervals of sulking. Giving pain to any creature weaker than himself seems to be his one idea of amusement, and he shows quite a remarkable talent in planning the capture of mice, little birds and insects."

Edward's hunting goes beyond mere child games. He is savage and vicious. This abnormal emotional makeup, linked with his physical deformity (remember the disproportionately large head) quickly drew Holmes's attention. And yet Holmes never directly observed the child, Oddly, the boy is never seen by Holmes or Watson on the night they storm Copper Beeches. Where was Edward while all the shouting and shooting was going on? We know that he was home, because Miss Hunter was supposed to watch him that night. Yet there is not so much as a disproportionately large head poking through the nursery door or a frightened scream when the shot is fired at Carlo.

There seem only more questions and no answers. My research would have stopped at this unsatisfactory point had it not been for a fascinating little volume by the Rev. Sabine Baring-Gould, entitled 'The Book of the Were-Wolf.' In it, Baring-Gould describes a trip he took to France and his conversation with a peasant near the village of Clyimpigyi. Baring-Gould wants the peasant to guide him back to the hotel. The peasant refuses, saying a werewolf has recently been sighted nearby,

"Picon . . , looked over and there stood the wolf as big as a calf against the horizon, its tongue out, and its eyes glaring like marsh-fires," says the peasant.

All of the local residents, including the village priest, told Baring-Gould that they were convinced the wolf was a werewolf. Baring-Gould, good Englishman that he was, walked home alone, unharmed.

The peasant's description stuck with me, until I recalled that it echoed Miss Hunter's description of Carlo: "I happened to look out of my bedroom window about two o'clock in the morning. It was a beautiful moonlight night, and the lawn in front of the house was silvered over and almost as bright as day. I was standing, rapt in the peaceful beauty of the scene, when I was aware that something was moving under the shadow of the copper beeches.

As it emerged into the moonshine, I saw what it was. lt was a giant dog, as large as a calf, tawny tinted, with hanging jowl, black muzzle, and huge projecting bones." The fact that both animals were "as large as a calf" alerted me to the similarities between Carlo and a werewolf. Note also the Frenchman's description of the "eyes glaring like marsh-fires," Miss Hunter describes looking into the outhouse and seeing "two glaring eyes and a vague figure huddled in the darkness."

These two threads, combined with the considerations listed below, have drawn me to the frightening conclusion that the "vague figure" was none other than Edward Rucastle, boy werewolf.

Consider the telling fact that Carlo and Edward are never seen together. Consider that Carlo only appears at night, and on a moonlit night which certainly has a full moon. Although Miss Hunter's encounter with the "vague figure" is in the day, she does not say she actually saw Carlo. That figure huddled in the dark is the child Edward, probably in some pre-dusk phase of his transformation from mad child into mad wolf.

Consider finally the strange behaviour of Edward's mother. "She had some secret sorrow, this woman," says Miss Hunter. "She would often be lost in deep thought, with the saddest look upon her face. More than once l have surprised her in tears. l have thought sometimes that it was the disposition of her child which weighed upon her mind, for l have never met so utterly spoiled and so ill-natured a little creature."

Little creature, indeed. Mrs, Rucastle's secret sorrow was the knowledge that her offspring was cursed to live a life of horror, inflicting pain upon other creatures in both his human and animal forms.

But Edward`s life was not a long one. Dr, Watson, no doubt unaware of the truly grotesque creature which stood before him, shot at the werewolf Carlo and killed it. No doubt the animal was immediately yanked from the injured Jephro Rucastle, who was swiftly taken indoors. The wolven corpse transformed back to the child after everyone was inside. Jephro learned of Carl's/Edwards death later, which no doubt lcd to his ultimate death.

For his own part, Watson deliberately made no mention of the werewolf, knowing that this part of the story would shock the Victorian audience. It would be interesting to know what his reaction was when he learned that his sure shot was actually a mercy killing, The good doctor put an end to the cursed baby of the Rucastle family.

This is an altered version of the original paper, delivered with great drama to the Cremorna Fiddlers of Williamsburg on March I, 1986. Despite the unanimous opinion of those present, copies of this paper have been made for distribution.

A SHERLOCKIAN TREATMENT OF THE MYSTERY

OF THE DEDICATION TO SHAKESPEARE'S SONNETS

Robert F. Fleissner

It has been surmised that Holmes would have solved the mysteries of Dracula, jack the Ripper, Dr. Jekyll and Mr. Hyde, and Edwin Drood._ Given the detective's far-reaching knowledge of Shakespeare's works, is it conceivable that he would not have indulged in deciphering the identity of the famous dedicatee to the Bard's Sonnets, Mr. W, H?

The issue was a hot one in Victorian times, as the copious Variorum notes reveal, and even Oscar Wilde reached his own idiosyncratic solution. Yet no one has seriously given a possible Sherlockian approach to this mystery of mysteries any credence. It is time to show how a Holmesian verdict was indeed possible.

In coping with this intriguing proposal, let us imagine the detective and his faithful *famulus,* Dr. Watson, engaged in a lively armchair conversation on the issue. Unlike most pastiches, such a re-enactment of a possible hunt for historical clues to a literary conundrum can be taken with utmost seriousness. The only bit of fantasizing permissible at the outset may be in determining why this dynamic duo decided to embark on such an adventure: perhaps they felt some kinship in the very initials W and H (Watson and Holmes)! After all, in The Sign of Four, after saying, "Give me problems, give me work, give me the most abstruse cryptogram," Holmes pounces upon the clue of the same initials, but in reverse, "H, W." He remarks to the Doctor, "The W. suggests your own name."

As all Shakespearians worthy of their salt know, the initials of "Mr. W. H." on the dedicator page have also been thought to be those of the poet's patron, Henry Wriothesley, in reverse for reasons of caution; nowadays, however, few textual sleuths take such an ingenious presupposition very seriously, especially because an earl would not have been addressed, even clandestinely, in such familiar terms by the printer. (For "Mr." throughout, read "Master.")

THE ADVENTURE OF THE WELL-WISHING ADVENTURER:

OR, HOLMES DISCOUNTS HOLMES?

"My dear Holmes! " Dr. Watson remarked, gaping at what he saw in print before him, "Do you realize that your name has been associated with Shakespeare?"'

"I am not a Baconian," the lank detective muttered softly. "The man from Stratford wrote the plays, no one else."

The good Doctor looked up, smiling.

"No one would doubt your ratiocination with regard to the greatest man in English letters," he purred, "But I refer to the sonnets, not the dramas. They seem to have been dedicated to a certain Master W. H., as you know, when they first appear in 1609. Now I read that a prime candidate for the dedicatee was named Holmes."

"A cousin, I believe," remarked Sherlock casually as if nothing would perturb him.

"Then you accept the identification?"

"Not at all,"

"Pray, why? I believe I am by now cognizant of most of your methods, but for the life of me I cannot understand how you can deduce a solution when all that is available is a set of initials. Surely you do not agree with Mr. Oscar Wilde that the allusion is to a certain Willie Hughes?"

"Bosh," said Holmes. He adjusted his calabash pipe in his mouth and settled back in his armchair. "Willie Hughes was a dandy, and although I am vaguely aware that our literary executor, Sir Arthur, believes in fairies - his Irish background probably being responsible-I refuse to accept such balderdash. No, Watson, the answer is much simpler. First of all, Mr. W, H. has nothing to do with the dedicatee for Shakespeare' sonnets. The initials were imposed by the printer Although it is true enough that William Holmes was engaged in the bookselling trade, a much more likely candidate emerges, namely Mr. William Hall. He it was, I believe, who obtained the poems for the printer, Thomas Thorpe, and so Thorpe alluded to him, a bit mischievously, in the celebrated dedication,"

The two detectors of crime were relatively at ease after a week of trying to apprehend the most dangerous men in Wales and Scotland, Outlaws still maintain their elusiveness, and so had some time to ponder.

"If the poems were obtained through the poet's family connections, a likelihood not to be easily dismissed, then Thorpe had reason to keep the identity of the dedicatee secret."

Watson appeared non-plussed.

"Would it not have been a compliment to both the member and Shakespeare to have identified him?" he queried.

"Ah, Watson, perhaps so, but if the poet did not wish to have his personal amours aired in public, and Mr. W. H. was responsible for surreptitiously getting them for the printer, the latter had good reason for not letting on who W. H. was."

"Are you so convinced that the sonnets were autobiographical? Shakespeare was a genius, as we know, and could have made everything up in them. Your conjectures are nothing else but that, sheer speculation, Holmes."

Holmes put down his pipe and looked intently at the dedication. He took up his magnifying glass and scrutinized the printing with great deliberation. Finally he gave a sigh of satisfaction and pointed to some of the letters in the facsimile.

"My dear Watson," he chuckled, "it is inconceivable that an author's life is not somehow manifest in his work. Are you familiar with the *tabla rasa* theory in philosophy? Your stare indicates that you are not. The point is that the mind is a blank slate until experience imprints its messages. Shakespeare, like all mortals, waited for his experience to influence him. Of course his secret life crept into his writings in some way or another! He wrote the sonnets long before they appeared in press. Evidently, he suppressed them for good reasons. But he did disseminate them among his private friends as is well known, and one of them gave them to Thorpe."

Watson pulled the ends of his moustache at this news. Holmes continued:

"Now, you will notice that the dedication is set up in a remarkable way. First of all, it is almost entirely in capital letters with full stops between each word. That is the custom with Roman inscriptions. Moreover, the lines are not symmetrical, or 'justified' as printers say, but laid out like a lapidary inscription. But what l ask you to notice in particular is that an extra-large lacuna exists between the initials of the dedicatee and the next word. Such a gap does not appear elsewhere in the dedication. To the keen observer, it immediately attracts the eye."

"Then why," interrupted Watson, "have scholars not noticed it before? They cannot all be dullards, you know."

"Precisely," said Holmes. "The question is well put. But the answer is readily ascertainable. The reason why scholars have not noticed this over-sized lacuna before is simply that it has not been reproduced."

The simplicity of this deduction made Dr Watson laugh too.

"Furthermore," Holmes added, "the lacuna is just large enough to make sense if we have a special reason for wanting it to. It attracts the eye; the printer must have had a reason. Certainly, he would not have been careless when the greatest poetry in the English language was at stake."

"If not careless," Watson felt compelled to inquire, "why did he indulge in such an enormous triumph? Was Thorpe an eccentric?"

"Very."

"How do you know that?"

Turning to his book shelf, the detective took out Sidney Lee's 'Notes and Queries? relating to William Shakespeare' and opened it to one of the Appendixes, that headed "The True History of Thomas Thorpe and 'Mr, W. H.' He showed his physician friend how Thorpe was an indulger in bombast, punning, and unusual wordplay.

And he mentioned, in passing, that Lee's name too was a hidden one, a pseudonym, Then he pointed out how Lee had read the familiar phrase in the dedication, "To the onlie begetter of these ensuing sonnets, Mr. W. H," as a reference to the obtainer, not the inspirer, of the poems. Watson was indeed impressed. But he pressed on,

"Holmes, very ingenious, I'm sure, but the verb beget means to 'give birth to,' and such a reading would suggest 'inspired.'

"Elementary, Watson," returned his friend. "It means that W. H. did indeed 'give birth to' the sonnets-but for the printer, not the poet. He gave birth to them on the printed page."

"Who, then, was the friend about whom Shakespeare wrote?"

"Ah, that is another question," Holmes pulled again on his pipe before answering. "Very likely he was an earl. And that is another reason why W. H. will not do as the inspirer. He is addressed as 'Masterf An carl was always addressed in print as Sir.' "

Suddenly Watson had a bright idea. Even he knew when he was inspired.

"Holmes!" he cried ecstatic ally. "I have it. Although not one of the more religious men in our Darwinian age, I cannot resist pointing out to you an example of the eccentric humour in Thorpe's mannerisms you have mentioned to me. The phrase which links 'begetter' with 'Sonnets' surely is a play upon words in the Nicene Creed. It alludes to 'the only begotten Son. 'An irreverent joke on the Bible, wot?"

"Exactly," replied Holmes. "But remember that the Creed also says, "Begotten, not made." The wordplay further emphasizes that the begetter was the obtainer, not the inspirer. Nor was he the creator. The notion that W. H. stands for William Himself is preposterous."

Dr. Watson turned to consult Lee's book again.

"Who, then, is the obtainer, Mr. W. H., Holmes? Lee seems to think it is one William Hall, a stationer's assistant in the printing industry. Do you agree? Or have you another William Hall in mind?"

"Quite. Lee was on the right track. But later on he wavered. He does not mention this possibility in his account in The Dictionary National Biography, you know. Consult the lacuna: 'W. H. All.'"

Watson appeared incredulous. "Can we even be sure that the first name was William?" he asked. "Couldn't it have been, say, Walter?"

"Doubtless," Holmes answered. "But the great majority of British men with the initial W were named William. Such a conjecture is based at least on the laws of probability. We are not dealing here with such a conundrum as the letters R-a-c-h-e, which could stand for Rachel but in point of fact the German word for revenge. What is more interesting, to me, is that our William (Hall, that is) was married nine months prior to the publication of the Sonnets."

"Are you insinuating, Holmes, that the wordplay in the Sonnets relating to 'only begotten Son' meant that Hall's own son was to be born?"

"Capital," rejoined Holmes. "Thorpe wanted him blessed with a son. This thought echoes Shakespeare's own in the sonnets, although the Bard was referring to his wish that his young friend would get married and settle down,"

"Do we know," asked Watson, "if the stationer's assistant William Hall had married and if his wife was expecting?"

"Indeed," replied Holmes. "William Hall of Hackney married Margery Gryffyn on August 4, 1608. The Sonnets were entered in the Stationers' Register on May 20, 1609, 'From fairest creatures we desire increase...'"

"But-but," blurted Watson, "was this William Hall the same as the stationer's assistant? Isn't that a long shot?"

Holmes was adamant.

"Church records will confirm that not that many William Halls were extant and none fits the bill better than the Hackney Hall, Hackney was not far from London. Moreover, records of marriage licenses confirm the relationship." What is of greater interest to me, however, Watson, is whether William Hall was related to Shakespeare's family. If so, he had ready access to the Sonnets and could have seen them to press when Shakespeare would have been least displeased."

At this point Watson appeared rather more knowledgeable than usual. "I seem to remember," he remarked thoughtfully, "that Shakespeare's son -in-law was a physician of some importance, Dr John Hall. He had a brother called William. Actually, the father was called William too; he came from Bedfordshire."

"And Bedford is not far from Hackney. Do we have any other information that Hackney was involved?"

Holmes seemed elated at Watson's medical ability to add to the investigation so authoritatively. A prime piece of such evidence exists," he said with great meaning in his voice. "Robert Southwell, who was a cousin of Shakespeare's and, for whose Meditations a certain W. H. again wrote a dedication in 1606, also had Hackney ties. He is known for having been at King's Place there."

Watson sat bolt upright.

"And the two W, H.'s could have been one and the same."

"You have it, Watson. The evidence is circumstantially, beyond reproof."

The two discussed the topic for some time. Other matters of allied crucial importance arose, such as whether Thorpe was in any sense indulging in criminal activity, To the question of his being a pirate-because the sonnets were published with numerous printing errors (evidently Shakespeare did not proofread them), were registered without his full name, and were, cunningly dedicated by Thorpe, who called himself a 'well-wishing adventurer.'

Holmes demurred. He felt that Shakespeare would have resented pure piracy, hut would have allowed for a member of his family, say a cousin giving them to the printer. After all, his mother had just died and so would not have been around to be offended by the promiscuous Dark Lady, True. Holmes had not much to say on the suspect of the mistress, but he finally appeared to define her as the Irene Adler type. The discussion did not break up until there was a knock at the door and Inspector Lestrade of Scotland Yard was admitted.

"We are grateful to you for your achievements," remarked the Inspector briskly. "But one mystery remains. The etymology or meaning of a name. This nomenclature, alas, happens to be my own. Would either of you two gentlemen tell me how it is to be pronounced? ls it Lestrade with a long or short `a'?"

At this disclosure both Holmes and Watson were total blanks, and the mystery has remained till this day.

Was Lestrade really that obtuse?

THE RHETORIC OF SHERLOCK HOLMES

Walter P. Armstrong, Jr

In a letter to George Sand, quoted (slightly inaccurately) by Sherlock Holmes in The Red Headed League, Gustave Flaubert writes; *"L'homme n'est rien, l'oeuvre-tout"*, the man is nothing, the work-everything. These words might well be applied to the master detective himself. We know his methods, but about the man himself we know very little; only what he himself has told us, and that is not very much.

We learn far more about him from the way in which he speaks and acts. Like a character in a play, he is continuously playing the role for which he is best fitted and which he knows best; himself. "You would have made an actor, and a rare one," Inspector Athelney has said. The stage's loss is our gain. For example, let us take one of his best known and most oft quoted phrases. It occurs at the opening of The Abbey Grange, As usual, Watson speaks:

'It was a bitterly cold and frosty morning during the winter of "97 that I was awakened by a tugging at my shoulder. It was Holmes. The candle in his hand shone upon his eager, stooping face, and told me at a glance that something was amiss.

"Come, Watson, come!", he cried, "the game is afoot. Not a word! Into your clothes and come."

Without question, reluctance, or hesitation, Watson rises and follows him. The phrase "the game is afoot" comes, of course, from Shakespeare's Henry V. Holmes frequently quotes Shakespeare, as well as many other writers ancient and modern, but I believe that his choice of this particular quotation is extremely significant.

In Shakespeare's play, the words are spoken by the King in his famous exhortation to the English troops before Harfleur, of which l give only the conclusion:

'I see you stand like greyhounds in the slips, straining upon the start. The game's afoot! Follow your spirit, and upon this charge cry: 'God for Harry! England and St. George!'

This is oratory at its best, a leader summoning lesser men to follow. As Sir Sidney Lee says in his introduction to the play:

'Broadly speaking, Shakespeare has in no other play cast a man so entirely in the heroic mould as King Henry. Such failings as are indicated are kept in the background. On his virtues alone, a full blaze of light is shed ... Alone in Shakespeare's gallery of English monarchs does Henry's portrait evoke at once a joyous sense of satisfaction in the high potentialities of human character and a sense of pride among Englishmen that a man of his mettle is of English origin'.

This description could with equal appropriateness be applied to Holmes himself. To us he represents the highest potentialities of human character and makes us proud that a man of his mettle is of our race. We do not presume to claim equality with him; we can only admire his superiority of character and intellect and, each time he demonstrates them, say with Watson, "Amazing!" and await Holmes's inevitable reply: "Elementary."

But it is not only in his selection of quotations that Holmes reveals himself to us. He was also capable of turning a phrase of his own. Father Ronald Knox, the earliest of all Holmes commentators, was the first to note his taste for epigram.

He writes, misquoting slightly: 'There are two specially human characteristics which come out at the very moment of action. One is a taste for theatrical arrangement, as when he sends back five orange pips to the murderers of John Crenshaw, or takes a sponge into prison with which to unmask the Man With the Twisted Lip, or serves up the Naval Treaty under cover as a breakfast dish, The other is a taste for epigram, When he gets a letter from a duke, he says, it is ' like one of those summonses which call upon a man either to be bored or to lie."

These are known as the Sherlockismus, of which . . . the following may serve as examples:

"Let me recall the incident of the dog in the night-time,"

"The dog did nothing at all in the night-time."

"That was the curious incident," said Sherlock Holmes."

And again:

"I was following you, of course."

"Following me? I saw nobody."

"That is what you may expect to see when I

follow you."

I cannot refrain from adding two of my own favourites. One takes place with an arch-rival Professor Moriarty face to face for the first time. Holmes is describing the scene to Watson and he helps improve its drama in retrospect:

When Holmes encounters him, he says:

"You evidently don't know me," said he.

"On the contrary," I answered, "I think it is fairly evident that I do. Pray take a chair. I can spare you five minutes if you have anything to say.

"All that I have to say has already crossed your mind," said he.

"Then possibly my answer has crossed yours," I replied.

The other is one of the few occasions upon which Watson, normally Holmes' patient foil, gets the upper hand with him:

"The famous scientific criminal, as famous

among crooks as -"

"My blushes, Watson!" Holmes murmured in a

depreciating voice.

"I was about to say, as he is unknown to the public."

The chief exponent of the epigram in Victorian times was, of course, Oscar Wilde. He and Sherlock Holmes were exact contemporaries, sharing the same birth year. Although at first glance they appear to have very little in common, one writer has described the Holmes Canon as "the dream-paradigm of the brilliant decadent, cunningly written from a non-decadent point of view; it transcends most of the decadent literature of its time." And Phillip Julian, one of Wilde's biographers, notes that "Sherlock Holmes and Dorian Gray might easily have met in a London fog on one of their respective searches for crime and pleasure." It is a little difficult however to imagine what they would have said to each other had they done so.

Much of what Sherlock Holmes says is not, however, epigrammatic but aphoristic. W. H. Auden and Louis Kronenberger in their foreword to 'The Viking Book of Aphorisms' draw this distinction between the two:

'An epigram need only be true of a single case - an aphorism, on the other hand, must convince every reader that it is either universally true or true of every member of the class to which it refers, irrespective of the reader's convictions.'

They then cite two out of many possible examples from the Holmes Canon:

'The more featureless and commonplace a crime is, the more difficult it is to bring home.'

'When you have eliminated the impossible, whatever remains, however improbable, must be the truth.'

Each of these statements is of universal application, as Holmes, who knew a good thing when he said it, was well aware, The first he used in slightly varying form in no fewer than six different cases, and the second in five.

Holmes had no compunction about repeating himself.

Finally, although Holmes professed to know nothing of Carlyle, he was much given to a form of speech of which that author is the acknowledged master: the apostrophe. I shall give only a single example:

'What is the meaning of it, Watson? What object is served by this circle of misery and violence and fear? It must tend to some end, or else our universe is ruled by chance, which is unthinkable. But to what end? There is the great standing perennial problem to which human reason is as far from an answer as ever.'

There are, of course, thousands of words attributed to Sherlock Holmes in the Canon of his adventures.

Many of them are highly quotable. 'The Oxford Dictionary of Quotations,' which the editors describe as "primarily intended to be a dictionary of familiar quotations," lists no fewer than thirty. Bruce R. Beaman, who accepts no such strictures, has collected more than 350 in his admirable 'The Sherlock Holmes: Book of Quotations.'

Based upon these statistics, Sherlock Holmes is certainly the most quoted non-Shakespearian fictional character in English literature. Sometimes he appears in unexpected places. To take two extreme examples, there are references to him in six opinions of the United States Supreme Court, and there are two, in James Joyce's 'Ulysses.'

The character who emerges from all this is not at first blush particularly likable. He is, at best, arrogant, caustic, inconsiderate, moody, disdainful, and selfish. How, then, has he managed to achieve such universal acceptance?

Joyce Cary writes:

'Holmes is the memorable figure he is because Conan Doyle grasped the essential truth that the deductive solving of crimes cannot in itself throw much light on the character doing the solving, and therefore that that character must be loaded up with quirks, hobbies, eccentricities.'

It is always these irrelevant qualities that define the figure of the great detective, not his mere powers of reasoning.

And Kenneth Rexroth makes this suggestion:

'Holmes himself is as wild a caricature as Dickens's Mr. Micawber. Yet we are as convinced of his reality as we are of Micawber's, precisely because he is an ironic caricature, like so many people we have known in real life who are more outrageous than any character of fiction.'

Holmes does not live in our world, but in a world especially created for him, and therefore he is infallible.

As the internationally recognized authority on semiotics, Umberto Eco, best known for his authorship of the novel The Name Of The Rose, says:

'Holmes on the contrary, never goes wrong ....just as he has the privilege of living in a world built by Conan Doyle to fit his egocentric need, so he does not lack immediate proofs of his perspicacity... Watson represents the unquestionable guarantee that Holmes's hypotheses cannot be any longer falsified.'

As T. S. Eliot has said:

"Perhaps the greatest of Sherlock Holmes mysteries is this: that where we talk of him, we invariably fall into the fancy of his existence." How can this be when we know that he is not, that he cannot be, real? The reason is very simple; *because we want to believe in him.* Holmes represents not the way things are, but the way ideally they should be completely logical. Our role is that of Watson: to verify, not to question, Holmes's hypotheses. Like one watching a magic show, we know that we are being deluded, but by a willing suspension of disbelief we accept the illusion as reality. And so, at least for the time that we are under its spell, it becomes reality for us.

Rex Stout perhaps put it best in a passage which I shall quote in closing:

'Sherlock Holmes is the embodiment of man's greatest pride and greatest weakness; his reason. I have heard he isn't even human. Certainly he isn't, but he is human aspiration... Man insists on nothing more desperately than that his emotions are controlled by his rational processes. More often than not, he actually believes it up to the edge of his consciousness. Rationalization of an action or decision dictated by an emotion is, indeed, a primary function of the mind. It is an ironically thankless task, since it must contrive the conclusion that the action or decision was itself reasonable and therefore no rationalization was called for. As homo sapiens, we resent with a resentment usually too deep or awareness, let alone expression, being constantly bullied by our emotions, not only in action or decision but also in the frantic search for excuses for them.'

To say more would be to risk the indictment which Sherlock Holmes levelled against Jonas Oldacre in the 'Adventure of The Norwood Builder':

'He had not the supreme gift of the artist, the knowledge of when to stop.'

THE SHERLOCK HOLMES COLLECTION

AT MARYLEBONE LIBRARY

Catherine Cooke

It is many years since the Borough of St Marylebone Council mounted the famous Sherlock Holmes Exhibition held in Abbey House. This ran from May 21, 1951 to September 21, 1951 when it embarked on visits to the United States and Canada under the guardianship of C T Thorne, librarian of Marylebone Library. The nucleus of the current collection stems from that exhibition and our Collection has now been actively maintained for over 50 years.

We attempt to collect all kinds of Sherlockiana but perhaps the broad categories described below will reduce the collection to more manageable proportions.

PERIODICALS. The Strand Magazine 1891- 1950, a complete run up to the date of Arthur Conan Dovle's death A large number of his volumes are here including of course all the Holmes stories except A Study in Scarlet and The Sign of Four. In addition, the Strand gives a wonderful source of material on all aspects of the art of the period covered. Authors such as P C Wodehouse and Sapper were regular contributors, and numerous interviews with the famous were published, often very well illustrated. A complete index of the Strand is in stock.

The Sherlock Holmes Journal, 1952- . Held here is a very nearly complete file of The Baker Street Journal. A good proportion of the American scion societies send copies of their journals and notices, and these are all kept on file.

BIBLIOGRAPHY. A very varied selection, most notable among them being the Gibson/Green bibliography of Sir Arthur Conan Doyle.

SHERLOCK HOLMES RARITIES. A representative selection, including a first edition of The Hound, oddities such as selections in shorthand, and several facsimiles. Another acquisition is the Len Deighton and Marvin Epstein facsimile of Doyle's manuscript for 'The Priory School,' published last year.

DOYLE'S OTHER WORKS. Not yet a complete set. Some items, such as 'The Coming of the Faeries' are held in photocopy only, and some of the very rare items still elude us, but most of his nonfiction and all his fiction but one collection of short stories are held.

(This excludes articles and introductions in other peoples' books.)

CRITICAL TREATMENTS OF THE STORIES. A pretty good coverage of what is available, including most of the "classics," such as Guy Warracks's 'Sherlock Holmes & Music,' and a large number of the more recent items, ranging from cookery books to O-level "crib" notes and London guidebooks.

PARODIES AND PASTICHES. All the Sherlock Holmes stories by other authors. Well, not quite all! Again, we believe we have most of the major ones, including books of the films such as Murder by Decree, John Gardner's Moriarty novels, and some oddities, teaching you chess or computer programming.

SHERLOCK HOLMES ON STAGE, SCREEN, ETC.

This section comprises both scripts (for example, the First Granada series and many from the Carlton Hobbs radio series) and criticisms and indexes of the genre.

BIOGRAPHIES OF DOYLE AND THE DOYLE FAMILY.

A complete set of the books as far as can be traced, and a good selection of articles and pamphlets, including works relating to Doyle's spiritualist campaigns.

BACKGROUND MATERIAL. Both fiction and nonfiction. Books which Holmes used, such as Bradshaw's Railway Guide and The Martyrdom of Man by Winwood Reade, as well as books on the detective fiction genre and the like. More a selection than an attempt at complete coverage here.

THE CULT OF HOLMES. A very mixed selection indeed!

Quiz and crossword books, badges, advertisements, a brick-if it mentions Holmes, and we can get hold of it, we try to!

ILLUSTRATIONS AND SLIDES, A large selection, arranged under the broad headings above. Particularly strong on film stills, Victorian London and other locations. Newspaper cuttings, mostly British and American, but with a few from elsewhere. Mostly the more recent years, but in places dating back to the early years of this century. Again arranged along the same lines as the book stock.

What sort of enquiries do we receive? A good proportion of visitors just want to look at the Collection to see what books have been published and what is available at that moment. Others come to refer to specific books or journals. A number of students recently have used the Collection as a basis for bibliographies required for course projects-we have examples of some of these. Several companies in the theatrical world have used us for research, most notably Granada Television. Publishers, too, are fairly frequent visitors, usually to gather illustrative material.

We also receive enquiries about illustrations from decorators and from private individuals who want reproductions for framing. We do run a reprographic service and can often arrange for photographic copies, the copyright laws being the only stumbling work in some cases.

This might be a good point at which to mention that the Collection is housed in the same building as two departments whose stock can be of interest to those researching Holmes. The Marylebone and Paddington Archives and Local History collections are the first.

They also have a wide range of material relating to London as a whole.

Rate books, census returns, files of directories, and large-scale maps of London are but a few of the categories of material held. The Archives

Collection also holds photographs and prints which form a useful adjunct to those held in the Sherlock Holmes Collection. Second is a large general reference library, useful for costume reference, statistics, topographical reference, social history, and the like.

The Collection is now housed in Marylebone Library, Marylebone Road, London NW1 5PS, which is open from 9:30 A.M. to 7 P.M. weekdays and from 9:30.A.M. to 5 P.M. on Saturdays. lt is, however, on closed access. For that reason, and since I am not always on duty, we do prefer people to make an appointment. This assures them that a member of staff who knows the collection is available. Anyone is welcome- either just to visit and see what we have, or with a view to more protracted research. People may look at the items in one of our reading rooms and may browse through the card catalogue. A printed catalogue and history of the Collection, 'The Contents of a Lumber Room' is available for purchase, price £5.00. Finally, should anyone be unable to come in person, we do our best to answer enquiries by letter or by telephone.

(This excellent guide to the collection was reprinted in 'The Sherlockian,' Vol. 1, No. 1.)

HOLMES AND WATSON

By C. Martin

You go together so well,

Warmth against cool reason,

The puzzled paired with

The solver of riddles.

The depth of friendship

Is ages old,

Yet hidden from sight.

The questioner, ever eager to be told

And the man of power

Who infers and deduces

From such small details.

The wonder of the one

Amuses, yet flatters

and sustains.

The audience with the magician.

The tricks are open to all,

But still remain unsolved.

"You see it all,

But do not reason!"

Your relationship is built on rock.

Your friendship will never die.

THE ORIGIN OF THE BASKERVILLE FAMILY IN DEVON

By A. G. Hunt

THE BASKERVILLE ESTATES may well date back to the Great Charter of Disforestation of 1204. Many Devon families can trace their growth from that time.

Grants of land were made to many peasant families in the thirteenth century. Slightly earlier than this, the second half of the twelfth century had seen the emergence of many Devonshire landed families, most of whom held their land by reason of knight service.

The name Baskerville suggests a Norman origin (Basque de Ville, Basqueville?), and maybe we should think in terms of a Norman descent for this famous/ infamous family. Basqueville in its turn suggests a Basque origin, which in its turn originated from the extensive kingdoms of South Central Asia. Fortunes waxed and waned over the centuries for the Baskervilles, support, generally being given to the Plantaganet causes whenever required. The fourteenth century was not a prosperous time following the Black Death of 1348 and the loss of much of the peasantry upon whom wealth depended. Copper and tin were both mined on Dartmoor at that time and may have been one source of family wealth, A further source of new wealth would have arisen from their farming interests in wool. As they were upon the high part of the moor, sheep and cattle were dominant and cultivation poor.

A change in wool taxation in 1362 was brought about by the important *Confirmatio Chartorum*, by which the freedom of the nation from arbitrary taxation was secured a late consequence of Magna Charta (1215).

The Peasants' Revolt of 1381, although spearheaded in Southeast England, was felt elsewhere, and the old Baskerville manor hall was one of many burnt down in that unhappy period of Richard II's reign.

Now, Sir Henry remarks to Dr Watson that they were dining where his family had dined for five hundred years. This implies that the hall had been built around 1389. It is a reasonable assumption now that the Baskervilles decided to invest some of their new wealth in building a large black granite Hall to replace the one recently burnt down.

Prosperity increased considerably in Elizabethan times. The North American trade grew profitably, a trade in which the Baskervilles profited. One of the more adventurous family sons sailed with Drake, Frobisher, or Hawkins on the privateering expeditions of the 1560s, swashbuckling ancestors of the wicked Hugo and later Rodger Baskerville, better known to us as Jack Stapleton. With this additional new wealth, the family extended the large twin-turreted hall by the addition of two new wings to create the Hall as it was in Sir Henry's time.

Baskervilles continued to live and farm in the hall, supporting now the Tudors politically, after weakly aiding Perkin Warbeck, the pretender to Henry V's throne. After this affair, in which they nearly lost their position, it became family policy to support the reigning monarch. Hitherto, as Yorkist followers, they had supported Lord Stanley at the time when he was aiding Richard III; Stanley's treachery at Bosworth in 1485 appalled them, and they remained quietly supporting the old cause and old religion of the Plantaganets. This support was later expressed by the adoption of Richard III's white boar emblem in the family coat of arms.

The year 1640-3 saw the family fighting again for the king, joining Sir Ralph Hopton as he led Cornishmen against the Parliamentarians in the West Country.

That they retained their lands after the Civil War was due partly to their isolation on the moor and partly subservience on the part of wicked Hugo's successor, anxious to restore the family name after his father's horrific death and disgrace.

At the time of the Restoration in 1660, family matters had improved to the extent that a Baskerville brother was sent to London to support the exiled King's cause. The discussions upon the Restoration took place in

Northumberland House, a strange coincidence of location when we recall that Jack Stapleton (Rodger) stayed at the Mexborough Hotel in Craven Street, which now runs alongside the eastern boundary of the old House. Doubly strange, too, that Sir Henry stayed at the Northumberland Hotel, now identified as the Metropole Hotel, built on land just beyond the bottom of the garden of this historic House.

The later history of this well-known Devon family is dealt with in a succeeding investigation in which the direct descendancy has now been established.

THE OBSERVANCE OF TRIFLES

By Grant Healy

MISS EDITH WOODLEY OF CARSTAIRS

All that is known about the Honourable Ronald Adair's former fiancée is contained in one paragraph at the beginning of The Empty House:

'[Adair] had been engaged to Miss Edith Woodley of Carstairs, but the engagement had been broken Off by mutual consent some months before, and there was no sign that it had left any very profound feeling behind it.'

The only mystery concerning Miss Woodley and Mr. Adair is this matter of a broken engagement. Why was it ended by "mutual consent," and why was there "no sign that it had left any very profound feeling behind it" (a situation, in my experience, as remarkable as the dog that did nothing in the night-time)?

Only by studying the character and habits of Ronald Adair, as recorded by Dr. Watson, can any light be shed on this dark corner of his short life. With this as my touchstone, I offer the following conjecture, Ronald Adair was a habitual gambler. Watson tells us that he was a member of no fewer than three card clubs, the Baldwin, the Cavendish, and the Bagatelle. It was at these establishments that he appears to have spent most of his time and a little of his "considerable" fortune. As Watson remarks, he "was fond of playing cards, playing continually. He played nearly every day at one club or the other." Not only did Adair play a few hands in the evening, he also took a turn of the cards most afternoons (as he did on the day he was murdered).

The Scottish-bred Miss Woodley would very likely have objected to her fiancé's obsession, and I can well imagine her constantly trying to persuade him to mend his ways and improve his company. She may have finally resorted to delivering the sort of ultimatum that runs, "Choose either your hand of cards or my hand in marriage. Ronald, you cannot have both."

If dear Miss Woodley did confront the Honourable Ronald Adair in such a way, conjecture concerning his reply, is unnecessary, The line "the engagement had been broken off by mutual consent" tells all.

LANGDALE PIKE

'Langdale Pike was [Holmes's] human book of reference upon all matters of social scandal . . . He made, it was said, a four-figure income by the paragraphs which he contributed every week to the garbage papers which cater for an inquisitive public . . , Holmes discreetly helped Langdale to knowledge, and on occasion was helped in return'. - The Three Gables.

What was the source of this "knowledge" which Holmes provided Langdale Pike, in return for useful titbits of social scandal? Surely, it was nothing that had any bearing on the consulting detective's cases or clients, as this would have contravened the impeccable code of conduct which he employed regarding such matters. By what other means could he have secured information likely to hold some appeal for the columnist?

It was unlikely to have been gossip collected at first-hand, as Holmes seldom attended social gatherings and had few, if any, friends in society. As Watson once remarked, "Holmes, who loathed every form of society with his whole Bohemian soul, remained in our lodgings in Baker Street, buried among his old books."

Wiggins and Co., invaluable as they were, were hardly likely to land themselves in many situations in which they could overhear anything remotely akin to society gossip.

There was brother Mycroft, but he seldom moved beyond the "rails" which constituted his "cycle"- the Pall Mall lodgings, the Diogenes Club, and his office in Whitehall. If he ever discussed his Government duties with his brother, it was hardly the sort of information which Holmes would have repeated, or Langdale Pike wished to hear. Holmes`s most likely source of garbage-press fodder was Shinwell Johnson, who acted as his underworld agent during the latter phase of the detective's career.

He would have been able to unearth a wealth of interesting town-talk during his regular round of "every night-club, doss-house and gambling den in (London)."

"Porky" Johnson was "on the prowl" during the Von Gruner affair. His mission, as Holmes said at the time, was to "pick up some garbage in the darker recesses of the underworld." He succeeded in this by tracing the fallen Kitty Winter and so helped to solve the case to a close, just one occasion upon which provided "information which proved to be of vital importance."

How many times did he provide Holmes with "knowledge" of a scandalous enough nature to present to Langdale Pike?

EXCLAMATIONS OF IMPATIENCE

"You don't mean to say," I cried, in amazement, "that that tottering, feeble old woman was able to get out of the cab while it was in motion, without either you or the driver seeing her?"

"Old woman be damned!" said Sherlock Holmes, sharply.

-A Study in Scarlet.

D. Martin Dakin, commenting on the above in his excellent book-length study 'A Sherlock Holmes Commentary', wrote:

"Holmes must have been a most controlled person, since here we have the only occasion, unless I am much mistaken, when he is reported as having used a swear word."

Dakin also mentions another occasion on which Holmes may have had recourse to bad language.

This incident occurred during the events of The Final Problem, to quote Watson's account of the matter:

"On the Monday morning Holmes had telegraphed to the London police, and in the evening, we found a reply waiting for us at the hotel. Holmes tore it open, and then with a bitter curse hurled it into the grate."

I would like to put forward the following as a possible third occasion, in which we see the great detective's temper master his outward composure, The episode in question comes from the original Strand version of 'The Resident Patient'. In later collected editions this passage was omitted:

"It was boisterous October weather, and we had both remained indoors all day, I because I feared with my shaken health to face the keen autumn wind, while he was deep in some of those obtuse chemical investigations which absorbed him utterly as long as he was engaged upon them. Towards evening however, the breaking of a test-tube brought his research to a premature ending, and he sprang up from his chair with an exclamation of impatience and a clouded brow."

Even if this "exclamation" were neither an oath nor a curse, it, at least, indicated that the Sherlock Holmes of 'The Resident Patient' was not a very patient resident!

THE SOVEREIGN, THE SQUIRE AND THE RED HERRING

"I was staggered, sir. I did not know what to do. I went to the landlord and asked him what had become of the Red-Headed League He said that he had never heard of any such body. Then I asked him who Mr. Duncan Ross but he answered that this name was new to him. "Well," said I, "the gentleman at No. 4."

"What, the red-headed man?"

"Yes."

"Oh," said he, "his name was William Morris. He was a solicitor and was using my room as a temporary convenience. . ."

"Where could I find him?"

"Oh, at his new offices. 17 King Edward Street, near St. Paul's."

I started off, Mr. Holmes, but when I got to the address it was a manufactory of artificial knee-caps, and no one in it had ever heard of either Mr. William Morris, or Mr. Duncan Ross."

(-Jabez Wilson, The Red-Headed League).

Holmes, on hearing the name "William Morris," made a long arm for his biographical index, and he may have found an entry (under "W" of course), similar to the following:

"William Morris, born 1834. Poet, author of 'The Earthly Paradise.' Designer of furniture, wallpapers, and stained-glass windows. Translator of Icelandic and Grecian sagas. Novelist, travel-writer and journalist. Latterly much involved with the British Socialist movement. Also, a major shareholder of Morris and Co. Current address Kelmscott House, Walthamstow."

The great detective would, no doubt, have commented that, not only was it curious of the conspirators to have used such a famous person's name, but that the staff of the artificial knee-cap factory had not remarked upon the coincidence, merely saying that they "had never heard of Mr. William Morris or Mr. Duncan Ross."

William Morris, the Walthamstow "revolutionary socialist," was never a solicitor. The nearest he came to that profession was in September 1885, when he found himself on trial, charged with the wilful damage of a policeman's helmet (during a 'freedom of speech' demonstration in Whitechapel). Morris was found guilty and fined one farthing!

In appearance and temperament, the flesh-and blood Morris resembled Doyle's Professor Challenger.

In the following, Bernard Shaw describes the Morris of the 1880s:

'Here, then, was Morris in his blue suit and bluer shirt, his tossing mane, which suggested that his objection to looking-glasses extended to brushes and combs, and his habit, when annoyed by some foolish speaker, of pulling single hairs from his beard and growling "damned fool." The disarrangement of Morris's (hair) was so effectively leonine that I suspected him of spending at least a quarter of an hour each morning getting it just right.'

Samuel Rosenberg, in 'Naked Is the Best Disguise,' comments on the use of Morris's name and links it with Oscar Wilde:

"(The) red-headed William Morris was undoubtedly based on the William Morris who gave Wilde his "ascetic antidote." . . . The extremely close friendship between Morris and Wilde is described in a letter written by Bernard Shaw to Frank Harris. Shaw, referring to Oscar's conversational genius and great personal charm says, "I can understand why William Morris, when he was dying slowly, enjoyed a visit from Wilde more than anyone else."

Taken at face value, the reported anecdote would seem to confirm Rosenberg's theory concerning The Red-Headed League (rampant homosexual symbolism, with thinly disguised portraits of Wilde and his circle).

Unfortunately, Rosenberg's theory does not bear close scrutiny. A glance at the dates surrounding the Wilde/Morris affair reveal it to be a "trout in the milk."

William Morris's decline began and ended in 1896; Oscar Wilde found himself in Reading gaol in May 1895 and was not released until 1897. Therefore, Wilde could not have read to the fading Morris, as he was a guest of Her Majesty's pleasure at the time. There is no further evidence to suggest a "close friendship" between the two men, or any evidence to show that Wilde have even visited Kelmscott House.

What we do have, however, is Morris's opinion of Wilde, recorded in a letter to Morris's wife, dated 31 March 1881:

"Did the babes tell you how I met Oscar Wilde at the Richmonds? I must admit that as the devil is painted blacker than he is, so it fares with O.W., not but what he is an ass, but he certainly is, and clever.'

Finally, a tribute to the late William Morris from the pen of his friend Bernard Shaw:

"With such wisdom as my years have left me I note that he has drawn further and further away from the hurly-burly of our personal contacts into the impersonal perspective of history, he towers greater and greater above the horizon beneath which his best advertised contemporaries have disappeared.

UNCOMMONPLACE BOOKS

Book Reviews by the editor.

SHERLOCK SLEPT HERE. By Howard Lachtman. Santa

Barbara, Calif.: Capra Press, 1985, $9.95. (Available

in the U.K. from Airlift Book Co., 14 Baltic St.,

London, EC1, price £7.95)

Howard Lachtman's study of Doyle`s American lecture tours is a welcome addition to the literature of Sherlock Holmes. In his lifetime, Doyle held America in a particularly high regard and as a young man made something of a name for himself there as the author of the Holmes stories. Lachtman carefully documents the author's four forays into the towns and cities of an awakening nation, providing some fascinating glimpses into the American view of Holmes. Two points emerge most strongly: the early mythological status of the detective and his creator's desire to be known as a serious historical writer, following in the footsteps of his mentor, Sir Walter Scott. Of all the sections, perhaps the last is the most remarkable. Doyle's passion for the occult sciences is seen by Lachtman not as the preoccupation of a credulous mind but as the culmination of a lifetime's work and the author's quest for verifiable truth beyond the material world of post - Darwinian science. Reading Lachtman's carefully documented account, one is made aware of the extent to which Doyle, in his later years, returned to the roots of the Catholicism he had rejected as a young man.

The book is a solid piece of research which throws great light on the creator of Holmes. My only beef is that the work omits to mention specific sources and is minus a bibliography - a minor complaint considering the high quality of the commentary. As a bonus, The Noble Bachelor is thrown in at the end (presumably for the benefit of the non-Sherlockian reader). This makes the work monograph length (some 139 pages).

THE COMPLETE GUIDE TO SIIERLOCK HOLMES

By Michael Hardwick.

1986. £12.95

ELEMENTARY MY DEAR WATSON: SHERLOCK HOLME$

CENTENARY; HIS LIFE AND TIMES by Graham Nown_

London: Ward, Lock, 1986. £12.95

The phrase that haunted the obsequious Prufrock - "And do I dare?"- might well serve as a comment on the present state of British publishing. Timorous, conservative, unadventurous, the giants that once roared for Rudyard Kipling, H, G. Wells, and Arthur Conan Doyle seem to be no match for the challenge of the Holmes centenary year.

Make no mistake. It is not my intention to belittle the work of the authors of 'The Complete Guide To Sherlock Holmes' and 'Elementary My Dear Watson.' Both have produced very serviceable guides to the Holmes phenomenon. Both books show a keen eye for design.

They are well - researched, appealing to the eye, and reasonably priced. The catch, however, is that they are cautious in extremis. In , the myth, they tend to miss the essential magic, the evocation of Lond. Of the two, Michael Hardwick's contribution is by far the better. An old hand at matters Sherlockian, Hardwick does justice to the legend and its originator. His style is lucid and expansive, his knowledge encyclopaedic, his approach scholarly. Each of the sixty stories that make up the Canon is carefully documented and introduced with biographical and bibliographical material indispensable to the collector. Plots are outlined in a manner similar to the author's earlier 'Sherlock Holmes Companion' (though this work far outstrips its predecessor), and these are supported by generous quotations from the text. There is a "Who's Who" of characters and an extremely efficient index for those who love the minutiae of the Canon. The publisher has not skimped with the look of the book, either. Bound in sections (there was a time when that was not quite so remarkable), the text is interspersed with many of the lesser-known illustrations by Paget, Twidle, Elcock, *el al.* The effect is most pleasing. Hardwick announces in his preface that "the higher scholarship" has been "determinedly eschewed." I thank him lor that, for this is primarily a most efficient reference work which will not only tickle the literary tastebuds of the novice but will also delight the *cognoscenti*.

Unfortunately, Graham Nown's work stands by comparison on far less solid ground. In his (and his publishers) defence, I must first express delight in the appearance of the work. No pains have been spared to produce that special "coffee table" look. Colour photographs, leaping from the glossy pages, cunningly augment the text. But it is the text with which I must take issue. The first 87 pages of this 143 page volume deal with the phenomenon of Sherlock Holmes. They describe the now well-known and well-worn story of Holmes's rise to fame and his creator's own success story. The style bears all the hallmarks of a professional writer: crisp, strong on narrative, entertaining. There are factual inaccuracies here, however (I counted four on a first read-through), and a quite unnecessary (and irrelevant) tendency to ridicule the efforts of those devoted to the "Higher Criticism."

Apparently the "handful of devotees" who produce essays of the type which appear between the pages of this and similar journals are afflicted with "tunnel vision." Moreover, Nown does not consider it worth acknowledging his sources, so that the fascinating tit-bits of information he has gleaned from contemporary sources could have come from anywhere, for all we know, (There are also several Holmesian works mentioned in error - e,g., a "book" entitled *The Final Problem*- (Where?) by Bryce Crawford and R. C. Moore. I have failed to locate the volume. Perhaps Nown is referring to an essay?)

The second section of Nown's volume deals with the personalities of Holmes, Watson, and Mycroft, and the location of 221B Baker Street. Here we are on firmer and more familiar ground.

The final section (some 40 pages) provides an entertaining survey of the Victorian underworld. This is perhaps the most successful section of the book. Nown's knowledge of Victorian criminology is varied, and the illustrations (taken from the Strand and from Arthur Griffiths's 1898 'Mysteries of Police and Crime' complement the text very effectively.

Altogether, then, this is an uneven work, beautifully produced but lacking in any real original research, or insight. One would have hoped for an index. Instead, we are given a glossary of Victorian underworld slang, a bibliography, and some footnotes. What we are also given is a pleasurable read.

SHERLOCK HOLMES: A CENTENARY CELEBRATION by Allen Eyles. London: John Murray, 1986. £10.95.

In their blurb, the publishers describe this handsome-looking book as "the first study within a single volume of the entire Sherlock Holmes phenomenon," referring to it as "a guide for devotees and beginners alike." Well, perhaps one should never judge a book by its cover, as the old adage goes. For, although Allen Eyles's study is refreshingly written and beautifully illustrated, it is by no means a study of the totality of the phenomenon that is Sherlock Holmes. It is, in fact, a brief and informative survey for the lay reader.

As a book for "beginners" (that word suggests the groves of academe, does it not?, The brief bibliography and filmography which adorn the final section would certainly fulfil that word- but a valuable guide for devotees it most certainly is not. There have been other more scholarly works than this, to be sure (Ronald B. De Waal's World Bibliography and Richard L. Grecn's Bibliography of A. Conan Doyle, to name but two), whilst the public image of Holmes has been most carefully and diligently examined in Michael Pointer's 'The Public Life of Sherlock Holmes' and similar studies. Nevertheless, as an introduction to the Holmes saga, 'A Centenary Celebration' provides an attractive addition to the bookshelf or Sherlockian Christmas stocking.

SHERLOCK HOLMES AND THE RAILWAYS

By Kelvin I. Jones

"You know that particular quarter, the monotonous brick streets, the weary suburban highways. Right in the middle of them, a little island of ancient culture and comfort, lies this old home, surrounded by a high sun-baked wall mottled with lichens and topped with moss, the sort of wall - "
"Cut out the poetry, Watson," said Holmes severely

- "The Retired Colourman"

There were two occasions upon which Mr Sherlock Holmes was brought to Lee. One was in the June of 1889, when he was called on to investigate the curious affair of the disappearance of Mr Neville St. Clair, and the other occasion concerned the investigation into the disappearance of the wife of Josiah Amberley, a retired "colourman" whose residence was at "The Haven" in Lewisham.

Dr Watson, it will be remembered, was called out one evening by a friend of his wife, whose husband, Isa Whitney, was known to have been in an East End opium den called "The Bar of Gold". It was here also that Dr Watson met the disguised Holmes and the meeting led to the opening of the adventure later chronicled as "The Man With The Twisted Lip".

Holmes chose the hansom cab for his sojourn into this town of Kent (it is academic perhaps that in the previous year it had been transformed into the administrative county of London). If he had taken the train from Charing Cross his journey would have been longer and more inconvenient. (Lee, Blackheath or Lewisham stations were available to him via the North Kent line. Borne on an extensive viaduct the traveller passed through the suburbs proper - "squalid alleys and clamorous streets gradually giving place to large market gardens" as the S.E. Railway Guide put it.)

The "seven-mile drive" from Swan Lane to The Cedars would have cost five shillings in Holmes' day and the shortest route covered would be six and a half and not, as Holmes tells us, "seven miles". The journey, during which Holmes tells Watson, "We have touched on three English counties in our short drive, starting in Middlesex, passing over an angle of Surrey and ending in Kent" would start from Upper Thames Street and the "broad balustraded bridge" which they flew over would of course be London Bridge. From London Bridge they would continue down Southwark High Street, turning left along Great Dover Street, and coming out into the Old Kent Road. They would then carry on into New Cross Road. From here they would turn right just after reaching New Cross Station into Lewisham Way.

Here Watson tells us "we had been whirling through the outskirts of the great town until the last straggling houses had been left behind, and we rattled along with a country hedge upon either side of us. Just as he (Holmes) finished, however, we drove through two scattered villages, where lights still glimmered in the windows."

The first of these two "scattered villages" can easily be identified as "Newtown" (no longer marked on modern maps), centred around Lewisham High Road; the cab would then come into the country once more with only a few scattered houses such as Llawrenn Villa and Stone House along the route. Then after coming out of Loampit Vale, the cab would swing round into Lewisham Road, thus coming into the second village of Lewisham.

The cab here would turn left up Belmont Hill and the cab's destination, The Cedars, would be on its left. It is worth noting that The Cedars still stands today, and its outward appearance is still the same as it was in Holmes' day. All that has been altered is the inside of the building. A newspaper report of the 1920s tells us that "Messrs Hodson propose to commence almost immediately the development of 15 acres, forming part of the grounds of The Cedars. The mansion is, we understand, to be converted into flats."

"It is worthy of note that it is proposed to retain the outward appearance of "The Cedars", the only alterations contemplated being to the interior."

Watson describes "The Cedars" as "a large villa which stood within its own grounds." A description of The Cedars as it was in 1888 one year before Holmes' visit, still exists, and we are told that "The mansion is scarcely seen until we turn a belt of trees and find it close at hand: and the approach at once reveals the beauties to be seen beyond.

"In the front is a border of the finest collection of rhododendrons, with the clematis virginian creeper and jasmine overhanging the windows in rustic form; and the venerable cedar of Lebanon, near the conservatory, at the top of the lawn . . ."

"Northward we look across the railway towards Blackheath at the head of the dell with the shrubberies at each side of the steep slopes which are dotted with trees; and include a fine plantation of the pinus Australasia and excelea of the Himalayas." That plant and many similar Himalayan species Holmes was no doubt to meet later, if we are to recognise his interest in botany. (Witness his words in "Wisteria Lodge"; "With a spud, a tin box, and an elementary book on botany, there are instructive days to be spent"). We are told by Holmes that "My room at The Cedars is a double bedded one". We also know that Holmes was "staying there while I conduct the inquiry". It will be remembered too that this was one of the cases that nearly foiled Sherlock Holmes, were it not for an all-night sitting in which he reached his solution "by sitting upon five pillows and consuming an ounce of shag".

The question has often been raised as to how Holmes reached his results, for there is no real explanation given at all. Mr Bernard Davies points out that part of the explanation may be that Holmes knew St. Clair through his acting days. But admirable as this deduction is it does not give us the answer to the question as to what gave Holmes the key to the problem. Mr Davies suggests quite correctly that "this was a case.. of some chord of memory struck by chance as in "The Lions Mane." " Now we know, and Holmes knew, that the name of the beggar suspected of murdering Neville St. Clair (and who was St. Clair in disguise as it turned out) was called Hugh Boone. This alias has its factual origins and although Holmes found that "it is always awkward doing business with an alias," the derivation of the name is easily discovered. A Boone family once lived at Lee "in an ancient red brick mansion, surrounded by a moat, in the Old Road, for many years called "Boone Mansion", and which was pulled down in 1824." However, the Boone family left a memorial behind then in the form of some thirty almshouses, built in 1826. These almshouses (no longer standing) faced Brandram Road, which leads d obviously have been aware of their existence as they were only into Belmont Hill, and which comes out almost opposite "The Cedars". Neville St. Clair was a few hundred yards from "The Cedars", and it thus was quite natural that he should gain his alias from this source.

The close proximity of these almshouses leads one to suspect that they also gave Holmes the clue to the true identity of "Hugh Boone". If he had seen the name, as is most likely, for he had been staying at "The Cedars", it may have well set off a train of thought in his mind which after the coaxing influence of the shag tobac and the Eastern divan, produced that rare outburst of self-criticism: "1 think, Watson, that you are now standing in the presence of one of the most absolute fools in Europe, I deserve to be kicked from here to Charing Cross."

The stationary type of begging practised by Neville St. Clair 1 was in fact much rarer than it is now generally supposed. Begging was illegal then, as it is now, and a person who drew a crowd round him in a busy thoroughfare was liable to attract the attention of a constable. The problem of begging in the capital had been partly created by the increased vigilance of the municipal police who drove the vagrants of the countryside into the metropolis. In the "paddingkins" or cheap lodging houses of the great city they could dodge the police much more efficiently and their anonymity served as an added protection. In the case of Hugh Boone, alias Neville St. Clair, he avoided prosecution by pretending "to a small trade in wax vestas". The competition was fierce and often vicious in those days. To succeed at begging you not only had to contend with the police; you also had to hold your pitch against competitors.

The procedure of "standing a pad on a fakement" (this involved carrying a card round your neck detailing your claim to charity, tragic past history, etc.) was at the best risky. The blind beggars (the genuine ones, that is) were best off. Gonorrhoea, for which there was no cure, and smallpox, rife among the lower classes, claimed many victims and the blind man with his dog became a familiar object of Victorian sentiment. Sham blindness was surprisingly uncommon, mainly because it did not often go undetected for very long. If the police didn't realise it, then your own kind soon would.

Boone faked a limp according to Holmes but "in other respects he appears to be a powerful and well nurtured man." Perhaps that was just as well, for he would have attracted little sympathy from his begging colleagues. But it was of course his appearance which drew in the money.

The return journey to Bow Street at 4.25 the next morning after Holmes all-night vigil would take approximately the same route as before. However, the cab would turn into the New Kent Road this time, and thence to the Elephant & Castle, turning off onto the London Road. At St. Georges Circus they would then turn into the Waterloo Road and as Watson notes "passing down Waterloo Bridge Road we crossed over the river". Here, however, arises one of those peculiar anomalies of unintended Watsonian misdirection, for we are told that "dashing up Wellington Street (we) wheeled sharply to the right and found ourselves in Bow Street". Now Wellington Street passes straight into Bow Street itself, the police station being on the right hand side opposite Covent Garden Opera House. What is unaccountable is that Watson should have thought that they turned right at the end of Wellington Street to arrive at Bow Street. All I can suggest is that the cab turned right into Martlett Court, down by the side of the police station, and that Watson, seeing the name of Wellington Street a few seconds before, assumed that by turning right they were presumably turning into Bow Street.

It was not until many years later that Holmes and Watson once again visited Lee. The Neville St. Clair case took place in 1889 and Watson did not mention the locality again (Except for a fleeting reference of the residence of Mr John Scott Eccles at "Popham House" Lee) until he chronicled the affair of "The Retired Colourman". Both Mr Gavin Brend and Mr W.S. Baring-Gould date this case as 1898. This is deduced from the information Holmes supplies: "Retired in 1896, Watson. Early in 1897 he married a woman twenty years younger than himself . . . And yet within two years he is . . . as broken a creature as crawls beneath the sun." It is assumed that Amberley was a "broken" man within two years of his retirement, by both commentators. However, it is just as logical to suppose that he degenerated to this state within two years of his marriage. This would fix the date of the case as 1899.

The identity of "The Haven" is slightly more difficult to trace than that of "The Cedars". Watson tells us that after leaving Amberley's house, he "had driven to Blackheath Station". Later we are told by Holmes that "it is only a few hundred yards to the station (from Amberley's house)". The station referred to could either be Blackheath Station or Blackheath Hill Station, the latter being nearer the centre of Lewisham. One is tempted to pick Blackheath Hill Station at first, but the station mentioned is specifically "Blackheath Station". A further objection to Blackheath Station is that it is in the village of Blackheath itself, and as Lewisham is mentioned as Amberley's residence the station that Watson would have come from was, one presumes, Lewisham Junction. In fact, though, Blackheath Station is just on the parish boundary line between Blackheath and Lee and by the London Government Act of 1899, Lewisham and Lee were united, forming a metropolitan borough. Thus Amberley's house could still legitimately be referred to as being in "Lewisham".

By 1889, Lewisham had become a sprawling suburb with a population of 92,000 people. Unlike today, however, it was still largely dominated by the middle classes. Men like Josiah Amberley were typical of the residents of this expanding borough. The station itself stands on high ground, "the fields (rising) abruptly above it to the top of the hill, and . . .

covered with villa residences and pleasant gardens. There are handsome and convenient district churches", remarks The Handbook of Kent . . . The "Grammar School", founded by the Rev Abraham Colfe, 1650 is on Dartmouth Hill, . . . and is in . . . the hands of the Company of Leather-sellers". It is in the vicinity of the Grammar School that Amberley resided.

Belmont Hill, which was then a narrow and steep country lane (now a busy main road) formerly had only three buildings: "The Cedars", The Rectory and St Margaret's Church. At the Blackheath end of this hill, however, originally stood a house called "Belmont" which was built in 1830.

An unusual shot of 'The Cedars,' Lee, fictional home Mr Neville St. Clair, and not far from the house where Jean Leckie lived with her wealthy father and brothers and sisters. (Author's collection.

This house would only have stood a few hundred yards away up the hill from Blackheath Station, and we can be tolerably certain that this is the site of the house to which Watson gave the obviously disguised name of "The Haven". The whole of the area north of Blackheath Station comes within the parish of Blackheath and not Lee, so the general southerly direction to which the house would have lain is also correct. ("When you have excluded the impossible, whatever remains . . . must be the truth" - Holmes)

Watson, being a habitual addict of the hansom cab, would have taken one from Blackheath Railway Station. We find in Butts Historical Guide to Lewisham, Lee, Blackheath & Eltham, 1878 the following information: "Cab stand - opposite Blackheath Railway Station for four carriages. T. Tilling owner. Stable yard adjoining with 15 other cabs". The close proximity of the cab stand would be yet one more good reason for Watson to go to Blackheath as opposed to Lewisham Station, for he could then indulge in his Victorian habit, while Holmes, whose efficient expediency is notorious, obviously found it an advantage to bundle the "writhing and fighting" Mr Amberley into a waiting cab which would then speedily conduct him to the custody of the police under Mackinnon, no doubt awaiting the arrival of their miserly guest at the station. There is also mentioned in the Guide a "pocket time book . . . published monthly, price one halfpenny". But no doubt Holmes was satisfied with his Bradshaw. Of even more interest, however, is the list of fare rates. In Holmes' day a twelve month first-class season ticket fare between London and Lewisham (and Holmes and Watson always travelled first-class) cost twelve pounds, which approximates to something like an eightpenny daily return fare.

The railways were not without their problems in those days. Blackheath 2, like Lewisham, was experiencing an expansion of population during the years of Dr Watson's visit and the pressure on the rail traffic grew in proportion. In 1877 the railway bridge had been widened to accommodate more trains. Lengths of sidings, stables for the railway companies' horses and coal yards for local merchants all helped to expand the area. By 1883 the Bexleyheath Railway Company was floated to build a line from Crayford to Lee via Bexleyheath, but the South Eastern Railway pushed them out. The new line was finally built between 1891 and 1895 3. In 1897 the station was considerably improved. Cast iron canopies were built over the platforms and the platform was widened. In the year following Watson's visit the station experienced a visit from no less an august personage than Queen Victoria.

As for "The Haven", the original building with its "high sun baked wall" as Watson described it, was demolished in 1907 and as there is an unfortunate lack of detailed description about the house in local contemporary guides and documents, it is indeed a shame that Watson was told to "cut out the poetry" just when his monologue was becoming interesting. However, it is of interest that this stood only about half a mile away from, and stood on the same road as "The Cedars". To Holmes at least, who knew this area, it probably brought back pleasant memories. Indeed, if he was as well acquainted with the area as evidence suggests, he no doubt knew Blackheath well and may, if we are right in assuming his eternal obsession with guides and directories of all kinds, have even had a copy of Bradshaw's Descriptive Railway Handbook of Great Britain and Ireland. (We know of course that he had the standard Bradshaw). This gives us an interesting picture of Blackheath as Holmes must have seen it

"(This heath) is now a favourite resort of the inhabitants of London who come in crowds during the holidays and summer season - donkey riding being a favourite amusement. The heath is exceedingly picturesque and commands several very fine views".

It is comforting to remember that since Holmes and Watson's day the heath is one of the very few landmarks that have survived the onslaught of time. But then for the eager pilgrim there is always "The Cedars" to visit!

THE HOUND OF THE BASKERVILLES

Demythologised?

By Robert F. Fleissner

THE MASTER SLEUTH and his cohort were busy munching rolls for breakfast when Mrs. Hudson brought in the morning paper, which Watson scanned first with interest.

"Look here, Holmes," he remarked after a minute's overview. "Someone has discovered that the Hound we were after had a Celtic origin."

"Curious, Watson," responded the lanky detective.

"But the beast was real, not a myth."

"But a monograph has recently been written on the Celtic mythology of the Baskerville Hound. Would not such an anthropological derivation appear plausible enough at first glance?"

"That is the trouble, Watson. You resort too much to first glances. In point of fact, the origin of the Hound from a non-physical perspective is bookish in quite another way."

"How so, Holmes?"

Holmes took a gulp of coffee and knitted his brow.

"I suspect," he replied thoughtfully, "that the beast owed its origin to its having been a combination of Francis Thompson's hound of heaven and Thomas Hardy's' Tess of the d'Urbervilles.'"

Watson was agog at this news, but he was determined to consider it critically.

"Come, now, Holmes," he said, "surely you did not think of that owing to the vague similarity between the names Thompson and Thomas, did you?"

"Certainly not," agreed his companion, a bit curtly. "My association is based on reasonable deduction, not merely coincidental sound effects."

The good doctor demanded further explanation.

"Very well," answered his friend. "Thompson and our literary executor, Sir Arthur Conan Doyle, had some close enough connections, both having been trained in the same place. It is highly probable that the latter knew of the popular poem 'The Hound of Heaven,' to begin with. "True," admitted Watson. "They both had some Catholic kinship, too, did they not?"

"That is neither here nor there," argued Holmes.

"Conan Doyle had left his faith, and Thompson was converted."

But Watson was determined to figure this out religiously.

"So. Thompson furnished Sir Arthur with a title. Our executor shifted the state from heaven to hell to make the animal more interesting, I suppose, is that it?"

"Agreed, Watson. But such a shift was. in itself. too obvious. His able mind needed a further connection. Hence, he got the final word Baskerville; from Hardy's d'Urbervilles. You might think of a friar's basket of herbs, if you like, in Shakespeare."

"Nonsense, Holmes! We know that Baskerville type was used by printers. There was no need to resort to still another literary precedent!"

Holmes gave one of his little chuckles.

"What has Baskerville type to do with it, except that the novel may be printed now in it? Sir Arthur needed a novel as well as a poem to go by. He recognized the stress placed upon Egdon Heath in Hardy's 'Return of The Native,' a desolate stretch of moorland; therefore he decided to take some of that dreary atmosphere and combine it with the caged-animal effect in Tess. And there you have the Hardy angle."

"Not very acute yet," added Watson, trying to be witty. "But what absolute linguistic proof have you got that a lady, being compared to a caged creature, led to the Baskerville Hound being cooped up? She did not do any howling."

"Perhaps not," replied the slim sleuth, "except in her lady like way, let us say. But she was brutal enough to slay Alex. In any case, animal imagery was one of Hardy's finest, especially in this novel, as everyone knows. Besides, we have a subtle clue in Thompson's own poem which provides a point of interest."

Watson rubbed his head in disbelief. He fetched a copy of the poem and put it before the sleuth, who then took his lens and examined the beginning (the print being extremely small, and not Baskerville).

"Notice the very first line," he remarked pointedly.

Watson borrowed the glass and read: "I fled him..."

"Does that make sense, Watson?

"Why, not really," the doctor conceded. "A word seems left out_ for proper syntactic effect: the preposition from it may enable you to apply a little of your deductive skills."

"I would dare say that that was _just a printer's error, or perhaps bad style, or at best poetic licence."

Sherlock Holmes could not help smirking a bit at this logic.

"Not bad for a sample of your ability," he said, courteously at last. "But you forget one more obvious reason: Thompson may have been inebriated when he wrote the line. You may remember that he had quite a problem with alcohol, and indeed was said to have composed this poem about his overcoming his alcoholic habits, symbolized by a hound, ironically, through religious faith,"

"My medical training makes me remember the case well," admitted Watson. "But, why, then, does he call the poem 'The Hound of Heaven? The ironic effect is misleading, is it not?"

"Perhaps so," replied the detective. "Yet I suspect that Conan Doyle was aware of it and applied the real hounding effect to the drug and hence to an unnatural stimulus. I am glad that you were able to get me the cocaine, Watson, by the way."

"But, really, Holmes, could not then both Thompson and our executor have been indebted to a classical hound of hell, namely Cerberus?"

"You still have not come to terms with the lacuna, Watson," returned Holmes, "Does not the omission of the preposition in the first line mean something else to you?"

"I do not see how the phrase 'I fled him' relates to your Thompson-Hardy effect, Holmes. I am afraid that I cannot accept your absurd explanation. I take it that you have been having me on."

His friend smiled once more and conceded that he had been a bit unfair in keeping the good doctor in suspense.

"Nothing could be easier to deduce, Watson," he finally said. "Our literary executor noticed the missing word also. He observed that the preposition called attention to itself by being deleted. He decided that one omission suggested another and that he would have to get his source of inspiration also 'from' another literary work. So he chose the Hardy novel along with the Thompson poem. it may have been an unconscious

decision, of course. Elementary, wouldn't you say?"

Dr Watson too was able to be amused when he heard of such ingenuity.

"You forget one thing," he ventured to blurt out at last. "Perhaps the Hound himself would have had something to say about such a matter. Why, he would have howled again, if he could, at your revelation, Holmes?"

At this point, Mrs. Hudson came in again with news of a visitor.

"Right on cue," said the detective, "Admit now, my dear, the one and only talking hound in our adventures - inspector Lestrade from the Yard!"

Knowing that Lestrade was one old dog who would howl only in the night-time, the twosome waited for their guest with equanimity. Perhaps he had a problem more practical than such specialized onomatology to bark about at any rate.

SHERLOCK HOLMES AND THE NORFOLK CONNECTION

By Kelvin I Jones

Conan Doyle set no less than three of his Sherlock Holmes stories in Norfolk, a county of which he was immensely fond and which he frequently visited during his busy career as a writer and campaigner. Doyle, who once owned a thoroughbred Norfolk racehorse, had already set one of his earlier Holmes stories, The Gloria Scott, on the Norfolk Broads.

Strangely, the inception of his later but perhaps most famous Holmes adventure, 'The Hound of The Baskervilles' began, not in the west, but in the east of England.

In the April of 1901, Conan Doyle, having returned from his adventures in South Africa, decided to go on a golfing holiday in Norfolk. Doyle had been demoralised by his experiences in the Boer War and had contracted enteric fever. He needed to recuperate. What better idea then, than to spend a few days with his old friend and journalist, Bertram Fletcher Robinson, at the Royal Links Hotel in Cromer, a place he had already visited in 1897 when he spent a week's vacation here with his wife Louise and son Kingsley.

We are informed by John Dickson Carr (and Adrian Conan Doyle) that Doyle stayed at The Royal Links Hotel in 1901, where he and Robinson hatched the idea of writing 'The Hound of the Baskervilles,' and that the two men did this sometime in March. Richard subsequently discovered that Doyle and Robinson actually stayed at the Royal Links Hotel in late April of that year, as a local newspaper, 'The Cromer And North Walsham Post,' reported. This date was also verified from the accounts notebook of Doyle, in which a sum of £6. 6 shillings for two days' residence, there. In fact, Doyle and his first wife went on holiday to Cromer in 1897 and knew the place well, as a letter from September 16th, 1897, demonstrates (p. 390, 'Arthur Conan Doyle: A Life in Letters'.) And as we now know, based on the revelations unearthed by Richard, in the publication, 'Radical Rethinks on Hound and Horse,' ('The Edinburgh Physician, A Lady and Mr Robinson,' Sherlock Holmes Society publication, September 2002), in the third week of March 1901, Doyle was in fact, screened off from the outside world, snugly ensconced in Sussex at The Ashdown Forest Hotel where he stayed with Jean Leckie, and his beloved mother, incognito, having booked the hotel without other guests.

Richard Lancelyn Green found another anomaly: biographers Carr and Doyle wrongly assigned the date of a letter written to Doyle's mother from Dartmoor as April 2nd 1901. The correct date was actually June 2nd 1901. We know that by the end of May 1901, when Doyle made his tour of Dartmoor, at least half of the MS had been written.

This grand hotel is no longer there, having been demolished in the 1940s, following a devastating fire, but in its heyday, it attracted the rich and famous to this luxurious setting. Today, the setting is equally tranquil, but a dense wood covers most of the hill over which the hotel once enjoyed its stunning outlook and the fields beyond are a popular walking place for local residents. A contemporary guide describes it in detail:

'The Royal Links Hotel, Cromer, situated on the heathery hills towards Overstrand, is the largest hotel in the district. It stands in its own picturesque grounds of seven acres and contains one hundred and fifty rooms. The grand coffee room, drawing room, billiard room, smoke room, and extensive lounge, all on the ground floor, are fitted with every modern improvement, while a hydraulic lift gives easy access to the floors above. In the grounds of tennis and croquet lawns, bicycle house, stabling for visitors etc. The Royal links Hotel affords an ideal hostelry for golfers and all lovers of scenery and good air. Adjoining, on the Lighthouse Hills, are the links of the Royal Cromer golf club, which for picturesqueness cannot be surpassed. The course consists of 8 holes. Within 20 minutes of the Broads, private steam launches to up to any number of persons can be ordered at the hotel office.'

Doyle, a keen golfer and all-round sportsman, had been here once before with Fletcher Robinson, enjoying a brief golfing interlude and this was his second visit with the journalist. The Royal Cromer Golf Club still exists.

Cromer pier today, much the same as it was when
Conan Doyle and his golfing friend, Fletcher Robinson
would have then known it.

When Doyle and Robinson arrived at Cromer railway station, in April 1901, cold winds beat the high cliffs and the temperatures were lower here than in the south. Robinson, who was a veritable mine of information about legends and folklore, soon began to regale his golfing companion with gothic tales.

In his memoir, ('The Chronicles of Addington Peace,' Harper, 1905) he recalled how 'One raw Sunday afternoon when a wind rushed off the North Sea,' the two men sat lounging in the comfort of their private sitting room at the Royal Links.

Robinson began to tell Doyle about the legends of Dartmoor, one of which concerned a spectral hound.

However, there is a very local connection to the hound legend. Both men would certainly have been aware of the East Anglian Legend of Black Shuck, for this was a tale which had its roots in the very place they were staying. But how did the idea come about?

There are several theories about this. A local story has it that one of the waiters at the hotel told the two men about Black Shuck, explaining that it was in weather like this that the phantom hound could often be seen patrolling the headland. He went on to explain that his own father had seen the beast running along the beach and became aware of its fierce red eyes. A second story has it that Doyle or Robinson may have picked up a local guidebook, a slim volume entitled 'The Norfolk Coast' which had been issued by the newspaper, the 'Norfolk News'. In the volume was the following curious entry:

'Old Shuck is the grimmest apparition of the Norfolk coast. He takes the form of a huge black dog with a single flashing eye and a mouth that breathes forth fire, and to encounter him is an omen of dread significance: it means that you will die before the year is out. It is, perhaps, the oldest phantom in England; it has haunted our lonely roads for centuries. Probably it is of Norse origin - the Black Hound of Odin - and came to this coast with the Scandinavian raiders. Its lair is some secret place known only to itself, but some of its favourite haunts are known, and not many years ago there were men and women whom nothing would induce to venture into them after nightfall. When the wind howled around their isolated homes, it was the baying of Old Shuck they heard, and they trembled in their beds.'

There is a tale told along the coast of a practical joke played upon some fishermen by an auctioneer at Cromer, now dead.

'Knowing that the fishermen would be leaving a house about ten o'clock at night - the hour suggests the kind of house - the joker captured a black ram, wreathed round with clanking chain, and kept it concealed behind a bank until the men came along the road. Just as they were passing the hiding place, the ram was pushed down the steep bank right into the midst of them. The result of this dramatic appearance of "Old Shuck" was a most disgraceful flight and no fishing for days!'

The third, and most popular version of events describes how Robinson introduced Doyle to the story of Richard Cabell (later to become the demonic Sir Hugo Baskerville). Robinson would have known of the story since he had a home in Newton Abbot, not that far from Dartmoor.

What really transpired between the two men we shall never really know. Some commentators claim that the idea for the murder mystery was originally Robinson's and that Doyle wanted to embark on a collaboration but later changed his mind. There is some circumstantial evidence for this theory. There are (curiously) three versions of the dedication of The Hound. The earliest states:

'This story owes its inception to my friend, Mr Fletcher Robinson, who has helped me both in the general plot and in the local details - ACD.'

However, in his preface to the 'Complete Sherlock Holmes,' Doyle later wrote:

'Then came the Hound of the Baskervilles. It arose from a remark by that fine fellow whose premature death was a loss to the world, Fletcher Robinson, that there was a spectral dog near his home on Dartmoor.

'That remark was the inception of the book, but I should add that the plot and every word of the actual narrative was my own.'

Which, then, are we to believe, and why the shift in Doyle's explanation? This inconsistency has provided the foundation for a bizarre theory, recently espoused by a writer who claimed that Doyle had poisoned Robinson with laudanum and did away with him. Sadly, however, the author in question overlooks the fact that Robinson actually died of typhoid. It does seem possible, however, that Doyle may have owed much to Robinson's ghastly tales.

We know, for example, that Robinson later showed Doyle the rocky outcrops of the moorland, the prehistoric dwellings, the gloomy walls of Princeton prison. When Doyle arrived in Cromer he had done with Holmes, having sent him to his watery grave at the bottom of the Reichenbach Falls. Since the tale first appeared in its book edition in 1902, following its serialisation in The Strand Magazine between August 1901 and April 1902, we can assume that he must have had a very quick change of mind about his detective.

Amid rounds of golf and long walks along the coastal path to Sheringham and Mundesley, did Robinson and Doyle merge in their combined imaginations the mysterious landscape of Dartmoor and the phantom hound of Cromer? Certainly, in the West Country Cabell legend there was no hound of hell.

The huge, jet-black creature with flaming eyes bears a great resemblance to Black Shuck. Several authorities describe the creature as being the size of a calf and the very origin of the name means demon, from the Anglo Saxon "Scucca" or "Sceocca".

Some say that to witness the hound portends death within a year. This fits well with the demise of the unfortunate Sir Charles.

Conan Doyle's description of Baskerville Hall bears an uncanny likeness to nearby Cromer Hall and it is my strong belief that Doyle had Cromer Hall in mind when he wrote this, for the correspondence is uncanny and contemporary photographs bear out this likeness:

'The avenue opened into a broad expanse of turf, and the house lay before us. In the fading light I could see that the centre was a heavy block of building from which a porch projected. The whole front was draped in ivy, with a patch clipped bare here and there where a window or a coat-of-arms broke through the dark veil. From this central block rose the twin towers, ancient, crenelated, and pierced with many loopholes. To right and left of the turrets were more modern wings of black granite. A dull light shone through heavy mullioned windows, and from the high chimneys which rose from the steep, high-angled roof there sprang a single black column of smoke.'

Significantly, also, until the great storms of 1987, Cromer Hall also had a Yew Alley - which plays such a major part in the book. According to local belief, during his visit to the town, Conan Doyle and Fletcher Robinson had dinner with the philanthropic Benjamin Bond Cabbell at Cromer Hall. During dinner Cabbell told them about his ancestor, Richard Cabell, who was Lord of Brook Manor at Buckfastleigh and had been killed by a devilish dog. It is more than likely that in 1901 the two men may have been guests of Benjamin's widow, Evelyn Bond Cabell.

When the two men finally departed the Royal Links Hotel, they went their separate ways: Robinson to take up a lucrative position as editor of "Vanity Fair" and Doyle to work at fever pitch on what he described in a letter to his mother as a "real creeper". However, it is curious to reflect that the Dartmoor hound may have had its origins in the legend of the hell hound Black Shuck. But then truth is often stranger than fiction.

NOTES

The once grand Royal Links Hotel was consumed by fire in the 1940s. According to one eye - witness:

'I Was There: Ron Jackson - a Memory of Cromer. Internet site.'

'In 1949 the Royal Links which had hosted Royals and the glitterati of the day was the first to fall to the contagious bout of fires which mysteriously began to sweep the area. Imagine that wonderful central staircase (with no fire doors of course) what a chimney that must have made. At some time during the night (it's funny how things seem to start at night) with the place unoccupied and no doubt the owners abroad, it went up like a torch. If you walk along the cliff path now, there is absolutely nothing to see of what had been a flagship hotel. The ballroom, which was situated lower down by the Overstrand Road in which they once made an early Come Dancing programme, on which Marie and I actually appeared on screen around 1961, followed its parent's fiery fate in 1978. I guess the site was worth more than the building and of course houses have replaced it.'

'Sun Aug 12th 2018, Jamie Leeson commented:

The ballroom (links Pavilion) became a popular music venue of the 70's hosting the Who, Thin Lizzy and I believe the sex pistols and countless others! There is a blue plaque on the building that stands in its place that is part of the Cromer country club.

A BIBLIOGRAPHY OF 'THE HOUND OF THE BASKERVILLES'

The majority of the books cited below contain references to 'The Hound' whilst some are entirely devoted to the narrative.

Baring-Gould, William S.

Sherlock Holmes of Baker Street: a life of the world's first consulting detective; by William S. Baring-Gould. New York: Wings Books, 1995. Hardcover. The first comprehensive biography of Sherlock Holmes.

Bell, H. W.

Baker Street studies; H. W. Bell. New York: Otto Penzler Books, 1995. x, 223 pages. (Otto Penzler's Sherlock Holmes library). Paperback. Reprint of an early collection of essays by noted Sherlockians.

Bell, H. W.

Sherlock Holmes and Dr. Watson: the chronology of their adventures; by H.W. Bell. New York: Magico Magazine, 1984.

Blakeney, T. S.

Sherlock Holmes: fact or fiction?; by T. S. Blakeney. London: John Murray, 1932. An early study of Holmes

Sherlock Holmes: catalogue of an exhibition held at Abbey House, Baker Street, London May - September 1951; presented for the Festival of Britain by the Public Libraries Committee of the Borough of St. Marylebone. New York: Magico Magazine, 1984. ii, 60 pages: illustrations.

Pamphlet. A reprint of the catalogue of the famous exhibition of Sherlockiana at Abbey House. Contains several references to 'The Hound' plus the famous simulacrum of the MS of The Hound.

Brend, Gavin.

My dear Holmes: a study in Sherlock; Gavin Brend. London: George Allen & Unwin Ltd, 1951.

Campbell, Maurice.

The Hound of the Baskervilles: Dartmoor or Herefordshire?; New York: Magico Magazine, [1983]. 9 pages: illustrations. Pamphlet. A reprint of an essay on the location of 'The Hound of the Baskervilles', which originally appeared in 'Guy's Hospital Gazette'.

Christ, Jay Finley.

An irregular chronology of Sherlock Holmes of Baker Street; by Jay Finley Christ. New York: Magico Magazine, [1985) A reprint of a classic study on the chronology of the Sherlock Holmes stories

Dakin, David Martin.

A Sherlock Holmes Commentary. Newton Abbot: David & Charles, 1974. An essential commentary on the Sherlock Holmes stories. Has a useful section on the dating of 'The Hound.'

Djabri, Susan Cabell.

The story of the sepulchre: the Cabells of Buckfastleigh and the Conan Doyle Connection; by Susan Cabell Djabri. London: Susan Cabell Djabri, [1990]. 15 pages. Pamphlet. A survey of the Cabell family and links to 'The Hound of the Baskervilles'.

Hall, Trevor H.

The late Mr Sherlock Holmes and other literary studies. London: Gerald Duckworth & Co. Ltd, 1971. A collection of essays on Holmes.

Harrison, Michael.

Cynological Mr Holmes: canonical canines considered: dog-lore and dog-love in the Sherlockian saga. New York: Magico Magazine, 1985. 60 pages: illustrations. Hardcover. A study of dogs in the canon, including 'The Hound.'

Harrison, Michael.

In the Footsteps of Sherlock Holmes. London: Cassell, 1958, illustrations. Hardcover. An investigation into the real world events in the lifetime of Sherlock Holmes, including an examination of places on Dartmoor referenced to the story.

Holroyd, James Edward.

Baker Street by-ways: a book about Sherlock Holmes. London: George Allen & Unwin Ltd, 1959, illustrations. A wide ranging collection of essays on Holmes.

Jones, Kelvin I.

The Psychology of the Hound. Penzance: Oakmagic Publications, 1997. Unnumbered pages. Pamphlet. Discusses the influence of Doyle's psychological state on the writing of 'The Hound of the Baskervilles'.

Jones, Kelvin I.

The Mythic Hound. Penzance: Oakmagic Publications, 1997. Unnumbered pages: illustrations. Pamphlet. A study of literary allusion, symbolism, and realism in 'The Hound of the Baskervilles'.

Jones, Kelvin I.

The Mythology of the Hound of the Baskervilles. Penzance: Oakmagic Publications, 1996. Unnumbered pages. Pamphlet. A discussion of legends of Hell-hounds in the context of 'The Hound of the Baskervilles'.

Jones, Kelvin I.

The Annotated Hound of The Baskervilles. Cunning Crime Books, 2019. An intensively annotated edition of the tale with copious and detailed footnotes, introductory essays, explaining the folkloric origins of the story, the exact relationship between Doyle and Robinson, the psychological aspects of the 'Hound' and the Gothic tradition into which it fits. There is also speculative commentary regarding Jean Leckie, the treatment of women in the narrative and an explanation of the symbolism in Watson's narrative treatment. The appendices include a large and comprehensive bibliography. An indispensable reference work.

McQueen, Ian.

Sherlock Holmes detected: the problems of the long stories. Newton Abbott: David & Charles, 1974. 227 pages: illustrations. A discussion of points arising from the four long stories. Includes a major section on 'The Hound.'

Powell, Virginia.

A Sherlock Holmes gazetteer: being an alphabetical compilation of the geographic references, both identifiable and disguised, found within the canon; by Virginia Powell; with an introduction by Brad Keefauver. New York: Magico Magazine, 1997. 157 pages. Descriptions of all the geographical locations in the canon, with identifications by noted Sherlockians. Includes Dartmoor ref 'The Hound.'

Purves, Shirley (ed).

Radical Rethinks on Hound and Horse; edited by Shirley Purves. First edition. London: Sherlock Holmes Society of London, 2002. 68 pages: illustrations. Paperback. A handbook for a Sherlock Holmes Society of London expedition to Dartmoor. Contains very useful detail about story locations.

Ross, Thomas W.

Good old index: the Sherlock Holmes handbook: a guide to the Sherlock Holmes stories by Sir Arthur Conan Doyle: persons, places,

themes, summaries of all the tales, with commentary on the style of the author; Thomas W. Ross. Columbia: Camden House, 1997. xi, 171 pages: illustrations. A guide to people, places and things in the canon, including 'The Hound.'

Shaw, John Bennett.

Collecting Sherlockiana: John Bennett Shaw's basic Holmesian library; edited and with annotations by Catherine Cooke. Cambridge: Rupert Books, 1998. 60 pages: illustrations. (Rupert Books monograph series 10). Pamphlet. A guide to the key works for the study of the canon. Very essential reading for anyone studying 'The Hound.'

Tracy, Jack (ed).

The Encyclopaedia Sherlockiana, or, A universal dictionary of Sherlock Holmes and his biographer, Dr. John H. Watson; compiled and edited by Jack Tracy. London: New English Library, 1977, 411 pages: illustrations. Hardcover. A landmark reference work on the canon, including 'The Hound.'

Weller, Philip.

The Dartmoor of "The Hound of the Baskervilles": a practical guide to the Sherlock Holmes locations. Philip Weller. First edition. Fareham: Sherlock Publications, 1991. 54 pages: map. (Franco-Midland Hardware Company share issue 3). Pamphlet. A guide to the candidates for locations in 'The Hound of the Baskervilles.'

A SUPPLEMENTARY NOTE UPON THE NAMING OF THE DEVON BASKERVILLES

By A. Godfrey Hunt

FROM NORMAN TIMES, it had been the family practice to name the first-born son after the ruling monarch. There were exceptions, of course, as in the event of a female monarch such as Queen Elizabeth I, in which case reversion was made to the forename of the earliest Baskerville, Hugo. The first occasion for this was in 1554, when a son was born just after Lady Jane Grey's nine-day reign had become known in Devon. In 1581, Elizabeth was on the throne, and the record shows the name Rodger appearing for the first time, possibly because the first-born had died after a younger brother had been named.

The third Hugo, who met his death at the teeth of the great Hound, was James Hugo. After the Baskervilles' sympathetic support for the conspirators of the Gunpowder Plot in 1605, however, it was considered wiser to play down the traditional regnal name and to use the second forename. The Baskervilles were not strongly religious and never really supported the Catholic cause, even in Plantagenet times, preferring the Old Religion sometimes associated with the Plantagenets and maintaining Pagan rites and rituals. It is interesting to note that there is neither chapel nor church within easy reach of the Hall, as was customary in those days. Even Grimpen was a hamlet!

The next and fourth Hugo was born in 1689, just after the accession of William of Orange. It was considered advisable to name this son Hugo William James, allowing a future use of whichever name appeared most prudent later; after all, King James II might have been restored! In fact, this Hugo, the legend writer, had three sons and a daughter, Elizabeth.

The first of his sons was properly called George in 1714 after George I, but he died in 1726, leaving Rodger and John to continue the family name.

It so happened that Rear Admiral Rodger Baskerville left no issue, and it fell to William to provide both the succession and the title.

In 1832, William Charles was born, coinciding with the last years of the reign of William IV. Upon Queen Victoria's accession to the throne, the use of William was dropped in favour of the second forename, Charles, out of respect for the late king. It was this Charles who eventually became the uncle of Henry and who met his tragic death in the Yew Alley.

As a final comment, the family crest, dating back to Sir William Baskerville, bears the boar's head symbol of Richard III and also a wild dogrose, This hints at both the legend and the ancient Greek belief that the wild dogrose could cure a dog bite!

HOUND TOR

By Kelvin I. Jones

All morning by Hound Tor the wind chilled my hand.

Such a day called for our hats and our capes.

Here on the rocks time moves like sand,

Carving the years into sentinel shapes.

In primitive huts a man might survive,

Crouching and freezing, cold unto death,

Scratching the ground to keep self alive,

Slipping fast into age, measuring his breath.

Hidden for centuries, things out of season

Lay here in hollows, gathering power.

No man who has sense ventures here without reason.

Where rock dips to bog land, sweet turns to sour.

We search while the daylight fades over meadows;

Out here is never a hope of a friend.

Darker, more deadly, the moor shifts its shadow,

Creeping behind us, hastening his end.

THE TANTALUS: SOME PAST MUSINGS

THE PAST YEAR has marked the centenary of the appearance of A Study in Scarlet and the literary genesis of Sherlock Holmes. To Sherlockians the world over, this is indeed cause for rejoicing, but what of the rest of the reading world? What of the occasional taster of the detective story or the eclectic reader who sometimes allows himself the indulgence of a goodly murder mystery? And what of that legion of writers who preceded and succeeded Sir Arthur Conan Doyle? To whom is owed the debt of originality? To put it another way, is Sherlock Holmes a mere isolated phenomenon (as Sherlockians would sometimes have us believe), a jewel in the crown of late-Victorian literature, or is he a culmination, a landmark, an extraordinary synthesis of ideas?

The publishing history of that first slim volume entitled Beeton's Christmas Annual need not be retold here. At first, it attracted little attention from the reading public and scant notice from the critics. Significantly, however, the illustrated weekly 'Graphic' wrote of it at the time: A year later, A Study in Scarlet appeared under its own title, carrying six dreary little sketches by Doyle's father. The critic for 'The Graphic' this time wrote: 'Nobody who cares for detective stories should pass over A Study in Scarlet... The author has equalled the best of his predecessors . . . He has actually succeeded in inventing a brand - new detective . . . The plot is . . . daringly constructed . . . There is no trace of vulgarity or slovenliness, too often characteristic of detective stories Besides being exceptionally ingenious, it may be read with pleasure by those [who] do not care for such things in a general sense.'

Was the writer of this review correct in saying that the work would "never have been written" but for Doyle's illustrious predecessors? And was he accurate in his assertion that here was a "brand new detective" and here was a "daringly constructed plot?"

Perhaps the most significant influence on Doyle's conception of the detective was Edgar Allan Poe, who, in three short tales of detection, created the psychological formula that has survived a century and more of variation and elaboration at the hands of lesser writers.

Disregarding 'The Gold Bug' (a story of mystery and analysis but hardly a detective story in the strict sense), these stories comprise 'The Murders in the Rue Morgue,' 'The Mystery of Marie Roget,' and 'The Purloined Letter.' Their structure has been loosely described by Howard Haycraft in his classic 'Murder for Pleasure' as: the physical, the mental, and the "balanced" type, respectively. It is, however, the very first of these tales which exhibits the features adopted by Conan Doyle, viz., (a) that the more outré the features of the case, the more simple is its explanation, and (b) that when all impossible solutions have been discarded, the residual solution shall be the only acceptable one.

Apart from the basic structure of the mystery and its solution, Doyle incorporated much more of Poe into his own conception than perhaps has been admitted by previous critics of his works.

The opening chapters of 'A Study in Scarlet' fascinate the reader with their vivid delineation of a Bohemian amateur investigator, dedicated to the doctrine of deductive analysis. The flesh-and-blood psychological realism of the work, however, is both an interpretation, yet an improvement on Poe's preface to 'The Murders in the Rue Morgue.'

Doyle's mentor writes: 'As the strong man exults in his physical ability . . . so glories the analyst in that moral activity which disentangles . . . He is fond of enigmas, of conundrums, of hieroglyphics; exhibiting in his solutions of each a degree of acumen which appears to the ordinary apprehension preternatural. His results brought about by the very soul and essence: of method, have, in truth, the whole air of intuition.... The analytical power should not be confounded with simple ingenuity; for while the analyst is necessarily ingenious, the ingenious man is often remarkably incapable of analysis . . . It will be found, in fact, that the ingenious are always fanciful, and the truly imaginative never otherwise than analytic.'

Poe's portrayal of Dupin as an analyst and a man of science, solving crime for reasons of intellectual pleasure, is a clear prediction of Holmes. But there is much more both to Dupin and Holmes than a basic ratiocination.

These literary figures (as has so often been demonstrated) are essentially projections of their authors' egos, heroes whose skill and imaginative powers exist to create a dramatic conflict in the narrative that must be resolved. Champions of mind over matter, expert reasoners, men of vast and often obscure knowledge, they are both to some extent superhuman figures set against the forces of darkness.

— Kelvin I. Jones

THE STRANGE CASE OF THE SOLITARY HUSBAND

By David Stuart Davies

Using the methods of Mr. Sherlock Holmes, it has become clear to me that one of the saddest aspects of the case Watson chronicled as 'The Hound of the Baskervilles,' was that of Doctor Mortimer's unhappy marriage. His wife was obviously an ogre who dominated the country practitioner.

Consider the facts. Mortimer served as House Surgeon at Charing Cross Hospital from 1882 to 1884. Holmes admits to having been incorrect in his deduction that it was Mortimer's lack of ambition that caused him to leave a prestigious London hospital for a country practice.

The detective, on meeting the doctor, comments: "You are an enthusiast in your line of thought, I perceive, sir, as I am in mine." Mortimer obviously had a promising career ahead of him before going to Dartmoor. He was the winner of the Jackson Prize for Comparative Pathology and had articles printed in the Lancet and the Journal of Psychology. It was, in fact, his marriage that brought an end to his prospects: "I married and so left the hospital and with it all hopes of a consulting practice," he says, with what we must assume is a tone of regret.

It was the domineering and selfish Mrs. Mortimer who forced this change, for he obviously had ambition and enjoyed the London life. He tells Holmes: "I usually give up one day to pure amusement when I come up to town, so I spent it at the Museum of the College of Surgeons."

What other evidence is there that Mrs. Mortimer, who, significantly, is never referred to in Watson's account, was overbearing and imperious? Mainly, it is her husband's avoidance of her company. Before the tragic death of Sir Charles Baskerville, Mortimer seems to have spent most of his free time at the Hall: "I saw a good deal of Sir Charles Baskerville... Many a

96

charming evening we spent together discussing the comparative anatomy of the Bushman and Hottentot."

Later, Watson records that, when he is staying with Sir Henry, "hardly a day has passed that he (Mortimer) has not called at the Hall." His actions are certainly not indicative of domestic bliss.

One can imagine Mortimer's pleasure at being able to place a further distance between himself and his wife when he came up to London to meet Sir Henry Baskerville. He brought his real friend and companion, the curly-haired spaniel, with him. This was probably because his wife would not tolerate the dog.

The fear she instilled in her husband can be deduced from his actions on his return to Dartmoor with Sir Henry and Watson. Once more within her circle of influence, Mortimer is too frightened to stay at the Hall, having been away from home for some time.

"Surely you will stay and have some dinner?" says the gracious baronet.

"No, I must go," replies the timid practitioner.

The death of his beloved spaniel may well have been the final straw that gave him the courage to finally leave his wife, for, at the end of the affair, Mortimer is planning to accompany Sir Henry on his travels: "Sir Henry and Dr Mortimer were, however, in London, on their way to that long voyage which had been recommended (probably by Mortimer himself) for the restoration of his shattered nerves."

Sherlock Holmes once observed that the countryside can harbour more dark deeds and cruelty than "the lowest and vilest alleys in London" and referred to "the hidden wickedness which may go on, year in, year out, in such places, and none the wiser." I believe that Mortimer's ignominious marriage is one such instance.

FROM AFGHANISTAN TO NEWPORT PAGNELL

By Denis Smith

I suggest that, as a long-time student of matters Sherlockian, nothing should surprise me, but I must confess to being as surprised as I have ever been in my life when I chanced upon the accompanying picture and description of H.M.S. Orontes recently.

In the first place, it seems remarkable in itself that, exactly one hundred years after Dr. Watson first introduced himself to the public with those three immortal paragraphs at the beginning of A Study in Scarlet which chronicle the events of his brief military career, it should still be possible to make fresh discoveries concerning these events. (To find something out about the Orontes is particularly interesting to me, as for years —until I read otherwise in the late D. Martin Dakin's book 'A Sherlock Holmes Commentary' — I had assumed that the ship's name was a fictitious one concocted by Watson or by his friend Dr Conan Doyle. In the second place, it seems doubly remarkable that such a discovery should be made in the little Buckinghamshire town of Newport Pagnell, a name quite unknown to foreigners, I should imagine, and probably known to most English people only because a service station on the nearby M1 motorway bears the same name. Yet it was there, in a shop which sells old books, cinema posters, bound volumes of magazines, and so on, that I came across the pile of old military photographs which included the picture of the Orontes.

I have read somewhere that both the Dead Sea Scrolls and the cave-paintings of Lascaux were discovered quite by chance, by people searching for a lost sheep or dog. I am therefore inclined to attribute my great stroke of fortune to the fact that I had our dog ("Bobby the Collie") with me at the time, although, to be honest, he never quite managed to get lost in the shop, was reluctant to go in in the first place (being obviously under the impression that we were going for a walk), and in fact assumed an air of utter boredom the whole time we were in there.

A British troop ship. Courtesy, Wikipedia.

Still, I feel that his presence must have influenced events in some mysterious way or other, for I had been in the shop several times before without finding anything which interested me.

The batch of photographs in which I found the Orontes had caught my eye as they were unusually handsome, and rather stuck out by their subject-matter from the surrounding piles of photographs of long-forgotten actors and actresses. They were hand-coloured in the old manner and clearly Victorian, to judge from the military uniforms and equipment, and were mounted rather nicely, ready for framing.

Whether they had been cut from a book, or from magazines, or had been originally issued loose as a set, I could not tell. Each has a title and description beneath the picture: "A Battery of Royal Horse Artillery on the March," "Pitching Camp at Aldershot," "A Field-Telegraph Party at Work," and so on, and each bears the inscription "J. J. Keliher & Co., London E.C."

H.M.S. ORONTES was one of the finest of what were known as Imperial Service Troopships. The Trooping Service consisted of five Indian troopships, the CROCODILE, JUMNA, MALABAR, EUPHRATES, and SERAPIS, manned by officers and men of the Royal Navy but paid by the Indian Government and exclusively used for the Indian reliefs, while the HIMALAYA, TAMAR, and ORONTES, with some smaller vessels, were employed for other relief work, both naval and military. The Troopers were abolished as it was considered inadvisable to keep so many officers and men locked up in ships performing duties which could be as well performed by hired merchant steamers. Troops were thereafter conveyed in steamers hired for the purpose, while the reliefs for men-of-war were sent abroad in modern cruisers, a system, which had the advantage of enabling the Admiralty, in case of a sudden emergency, to strengthen any squadron by the addition of these vessels, as they could be temporarily diverted to any part of the world.

Although neither the photographs nor the accompanying descriptions are dated in any way, it is possible to draw certain inferences as to the date and thus narrow the field a little. As the legend under the Orontes refers to the fact that she and her sister ships are now retired from their troop-carrying duties, it is evidently later than 1880, the year in which Watson sailed in her.

Further, one of the photographs refers to the Army Medical Department (in which, of course, Watson served), and, as the name of this department was altered to the Royal Army Medical Corps in 1898, then clearly the photographs pre-date that year. This still leaves as possible a fairly long period of time, and I regret that I have not been able to narrow it down any further. The only Whitaker's Almanack which I possess for the period in question is that for 1898, which gives a "List of vessels of the Royal Navy" as of the first of November 1897. Of the ships mentioned in the legend beneath the photograph of H.M.S. Orontes, only the Malabar and the Tamar are listed in Whitaker's, both as "receiving ships" (whatever that may mean), the former at Bermuda, the latter at Hong Kong. All the others, then, including the Orontes, had presumably been scrapped or sold by this date.

One final piece of information for he who has wondered in ignorance (as I had) where it was that the Orontes took her name. It is a river of the Middle East, which rises in the Lebanon follows a northward course through Syria and into Turkey, then turns westward to flow out into the Mediterranean Sea.

SHERLOCK HOLMES' ENCOUNTER WITH POISONS

by Raymond J. McGowan

Dr WATSON observed, in A Study in Scarlet, that Holmes was "well up" in his knowledge of belladonna, opium, and poisons generally. Holmes confessed that he dabbled with them a good deal. As a chemist dabbling in poisons, Holmes certainly would have become very familiar with the chemical analysis for the identification of poisons, as well as the physical characteristics.

The objective of this study is to determine why Holmes chooses to rely on the physical symptoms of the poisons rather than on the chemical analysis for the identifications of the poisons he encountered. This decision may have been based on the "state of the art" of analytical chemistry technique. The major poisons that Holmes encountered in the Canon were: chloroform (CHCI), carbon monoxide (CO), and alkaloids.

Chloroform had been known for the five hundred years before it was used as an anaesthetic. Its first use as anaesthesia was in Edinburgh, Scotland in 1847 by Sir James Young Simpson. As a matter of history, ether was known for three centuries but was not used as an anaesthetic until the twentieth century because of its flammable vapours, a definite hazard in the days when petrol lamps were used in the operating rooms! Chloroform (trichloromethane) is a colourless, volatile liquid with an ether-like odour and a sweet taste.

It is formed by the reaction of chlorinate of lime, amethyl alcohol. A detailed search of nineteenth-century literature has demonstrated that the only chemical test for the presence of chloroform was the "'Ragsky test" published in 1857:

The fluid to be tested for the presence of chloroform is introduced into a long-necked Florence flask. Into the neck of the flask is inserted by means of a perforated cork, a glass tube bent at right angles to the flask. The flask is then heated to 61.2° Centigrade (the boiling point of chloroform).

The vapours from the test sample will pass out the orifice of the bent glass tube, which is kept red-hot with a Bunsen burner. A slip of paper impregnated with starch containing iodide of potassium is held at the orifice of the glass tube. It will turn blue if chlorine is present.

A series of experiments was conducted by the author in his own laboratory to determine the practicability of the Ragsky test. This test is based on the fact that the chloroform is decomposed when it passes through the heated orifices of the bent tube in the Florence flask. The heated chloroform decomposes to form carbon, hydrochloric acid, and chlorine. Therefore, this test is based on the determination of the presence of chlorine, using the slips of paper, which are impregnated with starch-paste containing iodide of potassium as an indicator.

Chloroform lowers body temperature and blood pressure, produces toxic changes in body chemistry, and may damage the bladder and interfere with renal functions.

Carbon monoxide is a by-product of burning coal, charcoal, and auto exhaust. It is one of the few gases that has become very important in the field of forensic toxicology, because of its common use in murders and suicides. It reacts with the haemoglobin in the blood and converts it to carbo-haemoglobin. This reaction cuts off the supply of oxygen to the body tissues, resulting in brain damage and, eventually, death.

The first chemical test on record for carbon monoxide was in 1895 by J. Haldane of London.

Instructions were as follows: "Dilute the blood to be tested with four (4) times its own volume of water and add three (3) times the original volume of the blood of a one percent (1%) solution of tannic acid in water, shake well and allow to stand. Carbon monoxide blood forms a permanent light red precipitate - small particles that settled out of solution. Blood that has not been exposed to carbon monoxide will also precipitate light red particles at first, which will turn brown in two hours, and grey within 24 to 48 hours.'

The author conducted a series of experiments in his laboratory to determine the feasibility of the Haldane test. The results were negative, based on the fact, that tannic-acid precipitate also precipitates albumin (water-soluble protein). Therefore, the precipitate from the carbon monoxide would be obscured by the albumin precipitate.

Respiration is deep and difficult for the victim of carbon monoxide poisoning, and reddish patches of colour appear about the face and chest as the pulse rate increases. If the person is breathing, he usually recovers when exposed to fresh air and given stimulants.

The awareness of the alkaloid poisons came into existence in the nineteenth century, and they were classified as vegetable, animal, and synthetic alkaloids, depending upon their origin. In the countries that restricted the sales of alkaloid poisons, such as opium, morphine, and cocaine, poisonings were rare.

The countries that did not have these restrictions experienced many cases of alkaloid poisonings. Great Britain, for example, saw many fatal poisonings involving alkaloids. This situation resulted in an intensive search for analytical methods to determine their presence in criminal cases.

In their search, scientists found a method for the detection of alkaloids in their pure state. Researchers encountered analytical problems, however, if the alkaloids were contained in foreign substances such as food, blood, and body fluids. It was not until the 1950s that they were able to detect alkaloids present in foreign substances.

The general symptoms of alkaloid poisons are a period of excitement followed by drowsiness, weariness, loss of pain sensation, nausea, vomiting, pinpoint pupils, slow pulse, and fall in blood pressure, then death in respiratory arrest.

The results of this study demonstrate that the "state of the art" in the nineteenth century for the identification of poisons by chemical analysis was inadequate.

Therefore, Sherlock Holmes chooses to rely on the physical symptoms for their identification. Holmes's knowledge of poisons demonstrates that he had become very familiar with the pharmacopoeia during his stay at Bart's.

Raymond J. McGowan

NOTES

Works consulted.

1.   Gustav Schenk, The Book of Poisons (London: Weidenfeld & Nicolson, 1956), p. 183.

2.   Dr. Jul Otto, Detection of Poisons (London: H. Bailliere, 1857), p. 136.

3.   Dr. J. Haldane, Journal of Physiology 18:430 (1895), 20:521 (1896).

THE SUDDEN DEATH OF CARDINAL TOSCA

By George Cleve Haynes

PRELUDE

On a warm, Roman evening in the year 1895, two men met in a cool, high-ceilinged room. Marble abounded; the very floors were marble. The tall, heavy louvered shutters had been opened both to facilitate the flow of air and to allow the fading light to enter the room. It was the wish of its chief occupant not to increase the heat even by lighting candles. Although it was late September, the air was very warm. After some time had passed during which nothing was said, the visitor asked, "'Your Holiness?"

"You know the terrible news."

"Cardinal Tosca is dead," his visitor replied quietly.

"Cardinal Tosca is dead. But of course. All Rome knows this, and I this: the honour of the Church is at stake. I want an investigation that will reveal the truth."

As his visitor was about to reply, the speaker pushed quickly forward.

"For this you will contact a man in London. I have his address here."

"Of course, Holiness. And, his name?"

"El signore Sherlock Holmes."

"Of 221B Baker Street. I see..."

"See that he is paid in advance. He must be a businessman. And, of course, when word of this assignment leaks out, as inevitably it will, it will make his name even greater. Reduce the retainer that you have just thought to pay him by twenty-five percent. He will accept that. And tell him—I personally ask him to do this."

With a bow, his visitor departed.

I. LONDON: THE STATEMENT OF THE CASE

Rain fell heavily, cooling the air suddenly, turning the streets to foul mud. A coal fire burned in the grate of Sherlock Holmes's sitting-room in Baker Street.

Holmes, standing before the fire, was clad in a purple dressing-gown. Having removed his unanswered correspondence, he came across a note from his brother Mycroft. At the top it read, 'Draft of Secretary's Report, Annual Meeting of the Diogenes Club Trustees." The rest of the page was entirely blank.

"Singular man, Mycroft," Holmes remarked aloud, slipping his brother's communication into the pocket of his dressing-gown.

There was a knock at the door. "Come in!" It was Mrs. Hudson, the stout landlady, who entered the room.

"A gentleman to see you, sir," she said. "A reverend sort of gentleman," she put in.

"Ah, yes, Mrs. Hudson. Show him up, will you, please? I have been expecting him."

When Holmes's visitor had seated himself, and the preliminaries were over, the pair quickly got to their business.

'The offer is acceptable, as you know. So, pray, let us begin to have the facts."| "The public facts —"

"No, no. Please — the private ones!"

"Ah, yes, signore. Then, let me start at the beginning. Cardinal Tosca was a man approaching sixty years of age. He was born to a family of great wealth. He could have had any life that he chose to lead. He chose a religious life."

"Well, well,' Holmes remarked. 'As the Vatican demands something more than piety, what function did the late Cardinal Tosca perform?'"

"He oversaw banking and certain investments for the Holy See."

"Go on—please."

"He led a quiet life, becoming well liked when he accepted assignment to Rome. He made many friends. He had no known enemies. Yet he was stabbed to death on a street in Rome in broad daylight."

His visitor smiled slightly, "I was, at the outset of our interview, about to draw a distinction between the public and the private facts." Holmes waved him on.

"The public report was that Cardinal Tosca died suddenly on a street. One Roman newspaper reported it as an attack, and the Reuter's agency seized upon that to mean some form of seizure. But, you see, it was an attack by another person, who plunged a long, sharp, thin knife into Tosca repeatedly, killing him on the spot. Then —the killer hastened, though he did not run, away."

"There was a witness?"

"Oh, yes, signore Holmes. Cardinal Tosca was killed in the company of his nephew, signore Manfredetti."

"And this happened on a street, you say?"

"Si, signore. In Roma, a mezzo giorno. Noon-day, eh? The pair were on their way to luncheon. Cardinal Tosca had just completed some business for the Church and was to be the host to his young nephew, who had come to visit him from the family villa in the country." '

The prelate paused and sighed.

"Tell me how it happened. Omit no detail," the detective snapped sharply, sliding into the depths of his velvet arm-chair with his back to the window.

"To be precise, Cardinal Tosca was fifty-six years old. He had risen steadily within the service of the Church and at the moment of his death was a very powerful man. He oversaw the Church's finances.

Naturally, this leads one to wonder whether anything may have been amiss with the accounts over which he exercised stewardship."

"Naturally."

'His Holiness ordered an audit to be commenced - very discreetly, naturally."

'And the result?"

"Everything is in good order."

"Had Tosca enemies?"

"I have told you that he had not— certainly none that we know about. No man attains power without meeting resistance, jealousy, disagreement — but there is no clue which suggests that anyone wanted his death by unnatural means."

"Do go on," Holmes invited.

"On the day in question, the Cardinal had met his nephew, signore Bruno Manfredetti. They had prayed together in a chapel which was a favourite of the Cardinal's. The uncle was walking with his nephew on a public street in Rome, taking him to luncheon at a well-liked small restaurant near the Spanish Steps.

They were engaged in light conversation, as signore Manfredetti later told us. As they reached La via Campana, the street on which they were strolling intersected by La via della Scrofa. "You have been to Rome, signore?"'

"Yes, several times."

"You know it is very old by comparison with your great metropolis of London. In so many ways, more — er, rustic is perhaps the word—the streets, many of them, are cobbled and narrow, they wind even more so than in the older parts of your City. There are not the cabs, the vans, the heavy traffic of London streets.

"Moreover, this particular street, like a good many little ways in Roma, is virtually deserted much of the time. It is narrow, crooked, and good only for foot traffic, of which it gets little."

"And unlikely to possess witnesses to an assassination in the street," observed Holmes.

"Esattamente. As the pair approach La via della Scrofa, a man appeared before them, walking in the opposite direction. As he crossed the lane, he tipped his hat and spoke to Cardinal Tosca. He was Father Palombella, a member of the accounting staff that Tosca oversaw. The nephew remembers that the man was in a hurry but that the two men's greetings were exceedingly cordial—perhaps effusive, although they did not pause, but merely spoke in passing."

Holmes yawned. "Presumably each, having his own business, wanted to get on with it. What happened next?"

"Next—ah, yes," his visitor replied, seeming to have lost his train of thought momentarily. "Next is such a curious-sounding word. Ah, well, uncle and nephew proceeded on their way. The street runs about ten English yards of distance before it is traversed by another street. It was just at the moment when the pair reached the intersection that a figure emerged suddenly, running around the corner. It was a man who set upon Tosca with murderous fury, stabbing him several times to death. It all happened so fast that the nephew did not at first realize the import of the event, and, by the time he had, Tosca had fallen, blood soaking his garments, his nephew reeling in shock. The assailant had fled in the direction from which the two men had come."

Holmes leaned back in his chair, his gaze fixed intently on his visitor. "'Tell me what the nephew said. Everything that he said. Omit no detail. Something seemingly insignificant to you may be vital to me."

The priest thought for a moment, then began to speak again in slower, more measured phrases.

"Understand that I am translating everything."

Holmes nodded.

"The nephew, when questioned by the police, and again later by myself, alone, recounted the same event. You have already heard most of what he said. Let me think . . . oh, yes, he did say that when the assassin set upon his uncle, it appeared as if the victim were about to embrace his attacker. I thought that strange. He described the killer as being tall, well-built, wearing dark clothes and a long, hooded garment— what you call a cape — over all, which concealed his features, and the fact that he grasped a knife, until it was too late. Once having stabbed Tosca to death, he fled on foot, never more to be seen."

"How very dramatic."

"An ugly drama," the cleric remarked.

'Who came upon the scene? How did the nephew summon help?"

"Palombella came upon the scene, as you put it. Done with the very brief business he had transacted — he had in fact only taken the route as a short-cut to a tabaccheria to purchase stamps —he was on his way back to the Church finance office's meeting with a representative of the French bank when he came upon the body of his friend. Signore Manfredetti, the deceased's nephew, having recovered himself so far as to realize the urgent necessity of summoning help, begged of Cardinal Palombella to deliver the last rites while he, Manfredetti, went off in the direction of the great Corso, where he raised the cry of murder."

"Having reached the end of his narrative with no great final observation, nor any reaction from his hearer, whose head was sunk against the cushion of his arm-chair and whose eyes were closed, the Cardinal sat with open hands spread wide apart, palms up and a look of growing curiosity on his face as he regarded the laconic detective. A long silence ensued.

II. EXCERPT FROM THE DIARY OF DR. WATSON

While I was out, Holmes received a visitor from Rome.

A certain Cardinal Rici called to lay before my friend the facts in the sudden death of Cardinal Tosca.

Holmes had recounted the known facts to me. He did this at tea this afternoon.

"Surely," I remarked, "there is no solution to this crime.

'Why do you say that, Watson?" asked he, pushing away his tea cup to reach for his cherrywood pipe. "It was a random event. Someone emerged from the Roman crowd, someone wearing a hooded garment, plunged a knife into the man, then vanished. The only witness failed to observe any recognisable features!

"How on earth can you make anything out of that?"

"Well, my dear Watson, as you state the case, it does not seem very favourable for solution. And yet there are one or two points."

"I would be glad if you were to share them with me."

Holmes sent a great blue cloud of smoke rising toward the ceiling.

"To begin with, the killer was someone whom Tosca knew. Do you seem startled? Consider. If it were a political assassination, there would need to be a political motive. None is known. No anarchist or anti-cleric has claimed the deed, when enough time has surely passed for such an announcement. No, I think it reasonable to conclude that the crime was committed by an acquaintance. What was the nephew's testimony? His uncle seemed to be about to embrace his attacker. That would make perfect sense if the attacker were known to the victim, who recognized him but did not perceive the attack coming. Of course, in so reasoning, we discard the emerging- official theory."

"Oh?" I queried. "I was not aware that the Roman authorities had any theory."

For reply, Holmes tossed a telegram to me. It was dated that same day and ran this way:

'Bruno Manfredetti inherits his mother's vast estates owing to the death of his uncle. Rome police have arrested him.'

"Cardinal Rici apparently was informed upon returning to his lodging, and he in turn sent this telegram to me."

"You believe the nephew did not procure his uncle's murder?'"

"Of course, Watson. He would be a very foolish man indeed to stage such a dramatic event. Should such a motive be at hand, some other means of dispatch would surely have been desirable. Poison, |perhaps, or an unseen murder, the body floating in the Tiber. But now an attack by a hooded figure in broad daylight in the nephew's presence. It is too much of La Scala, really!"

"The Rome police believe it," I rejoined.

"Hah!" Holmes retorted. "Miserable bunglers. Would that life were so simple."

There came the sound of the bell from below, followed a short time later by the sound of our housekeeper's approach, ending with a rap on our door.

"Come in, Mrs. Hudson!" cried Holmes. "What have we here?"

"This came for you by messenger, Mr. Holmes," the good lady said, placing a small parcel on the table.

"Thank you, Mrs. Hudson. Well, Watson, if you will pardon me, I wish to free myself from the inclemency of our British climate to stroll for an hour or two along the warm streets of a more leisurely southern city. For this liberation, I require total silence, and you will not mind if I smoke," said he, tearing open the package to reveal a thick map, folded over many times.

"This," he added, taking his seat in our bow window, "gives us an intellectual journey through the winding Le vie di Roma."

For my part, I had some necessity of work at my desk and took advantage of the silence which Holmes imposed upon himself to balance my cheque book.

But, as my companion continued to recharge his pipe, bowl after bowl, and as our little room filled with the acrid smoke of his shag tobacco, I found myself about dusk reaching for my hat and stick to stroll the street in search of some fresh air. I turned the corner at Blandford Street, passed through Gloucester Place and so into Bryanston Square and those quiet ways that lie west of Baker Street in the general direction of the Edgware Road.

III, LETTER OF POPE LEO XIII TO SHERLOCK HOLMES

Dear Mr. Holmes —

No one knows better than ourself the remarkable gifts which you possess, and the good works which you have done with them. The affair of our Vatican cameos stands shining in memory as an example of your great reasoning skills. So it was that you were the only man to be entrusted with this present, dark, sordid mystery.

This present letter bears our Papal seal, and will be hand-carried to you by a trusted servant, who is our close cousin, bound by an oath of secrecy not to disclose his mission to anyone but yourself. You should know as much as ourself about the people involved in this case. In addition, troubling facts have come to light. These, too, will we lay before you in this secret missive.

The murderer's victim, our lately beloved brother, the Cardinal Tosca, was a man of great talent. He was good with figures; he understood finances and got along well with men of practical affairs. The finances of the Church are complex, and Cardinal Tosca bore the burden of them. He held his position since 1878 and to some extent created it in its present form. After ourself, Cardinal Tosca controlled the Church's finances.

Following his death, we ordered a special audit to be made of certain accounts, some selected for specific reasons, others at random. We thought it prudent to study these matters as possibly furnishing some clue to the terrible event that occurred recently. The preliminary audit revealed no discrepancies. Cardinal Rici, who consults you at our request, knows of it. What he does not know is that further audit has revealed a scandalous problem. Systematically, and in the most sophisticated way imaginable, there has been a slight siphoning-off of interest on certain accounts. This has, so far as can be presently determined, taken place regularly over the past four years. The total amounts involved, especially when one considers the accruing interest yielded by their potential re-investment, totals several fortunes. The trail leads to Switzerland where it ends, for requests to the banks involved were utterly of no avail. They will not yield any particle of information. Who may have been responsible for these thefts is completely uncertain.

Apart from Cardinal Tosca, three others occupy the stage in the unfolding drama of his death. One is his nephew, signore Manfredetti, another is Cardinal Palombella, and the third is Cardinal Rici with whom you have now met. What we can tell you about each of these men sheds no light upon the problem from our boulevard assassin who flees. That is much less demanding upon the powers of the imagination than the blow of an unseen hand, which invites an even more open-ended speculation as to his identity.

"Let me return to the hypothesis that this Cardinal Rici might have wanted to embarrass Cardinal Tosca. The nephew would not very much care about scandal, I think, if he were involved in the plot. His motive would be to get his hands on the money. It would not matter to him if that money were tainted. He would want it to spend. Could it be that he and Rici agreed upon a plan which would embarrass his uncle, and of course any one of the family who cared, thereby satisfying Rict's goals while the nephew should take the money? Manfredetti could then go where he wanted, oblivious to scandal. As for this man Palombello, he stood to gain a powerful position. I have said that. As I have thought about the case, Holmes, it seems to me that Palombello could be a third conspirator. It was he who provided a corroboration of the young man's story. That is a pretty sordid state of affairs, if it is true, but it all fits. I believe that a case can be made that all three are conspirators in the murder of Cardinal Tosca."

Sherlock Holmes sat in silence for a long time.

'Well, my dear Watson, your solution of the case is a remarkable tour de force. 1 am amazed," said he.

He rose from his chair and walked to the window, from which he stared down at the stream of traffic in Baker Street.

"I am continually amazed at the ingenuity of man for wickedness. You have become the raven of crime, dear Watson, picking away as greedily at the corpse as any other feeder on carrion. Oh, I go too far. Do forgive me."

I laughed at my friend's simile. 'Holmes, you do go a bit far at times. But the question is whether I have cleaned the facts down to the bone.'"

It was Holmes's turn to chuckle. "'So much so that you have missed the truth, I am afraid."

After the attentive, and I may say eager, reception of my explanation, these words came as a great shock to me. When I had absorbed them, I was able to say, "Well, Holmes, I am waiting."

"You are a great chronicler, Watson. You have set out very neatly what is passed," he said, indicating the open copy of the Strand. "'What is past is prologue,' as the poet has it. In this case, what is past is the pre-eminent criminal career of the late but unlamented Professor Moriarty. Moriarty was a very forward looking man. Being a mathematician, he was a schemer by nature. Planning was essential to the success of his enterprise. You put it down so well, my dear fellow."

Holmes took up the periodical and read:

"The cleverest rogue and the most powerful syndicate of criminals in Europe." He handed the text to me.

"I looked that up just now. In about 1890, as I reconstruct it, Moriarty saw an opportunity to place a man, an imposter, in the Vatican. This would be very useful to him. An imposter of the Moriarty crime syndicate assumed the identity of an obscure but talented monsignor who had recently obtained his position. He was not very well known outside of a small circle of elderly men. This made things very convenient indeed. This man worked his way to higher offices, to Rome and into finance in 1891. In that year, of course, as we know, Moriarty's career abruptly ended in Switzerland. It was in that year that the sophisticated theft scheme began to pour money into the Swiss banks. If Tosca could be gotten out of the way, then the imposter would have great power in addition to personal wealth. The basic scheme, as originally crafted by that great master of evil, Professor Moriarty, was as bold as it was simple. I am speaking of the man who calls himself Cardinal Palombello. In reality, this Palombello is an imposter, and in the first instance no cleric at all. My immediate suspicion was raised by the fact that the nephew had to ask him to pray over Tosca. A true priest would have been gravely concerned about the matter. Oh, yes, Cardinal Tosca was indeed murdered in a Roman street in the presence of his nephew. Coincidentally, Cardinal Rici was nearby but had no knowledge of the crime. Rici is a careful man. Had he been involved in the murder, you can be sure he would have explained his presence, not leaving it to chance, and to the. arousal of suspicion, that his proximity to the crime should be found out. I will tell you how Palombello murdered Cardinal Tosca.

"Tosca and his nephew were walking more or less in an easterly direction. Palombello approached them from the opposite direction. It is true that Palombello was on his way to a tobacconist's, where he did buy stamps, but he did not buy them until after the murder was committed. It would be highly unusual for such a casual transaction to result in the tobacconist or anyone who chanced to be in his shop noting the exact time o'clock. Even so, clocks can be unsynchronized, and it is most likely that Palombello knew which shop he was going to, where the proprietor would likely be a weary fellow uninterested in the precise time. Palombello walked down the street, no doubt hurrying the final few steps after sighting the body of Tosca and the frightened, bewildered nephew."

"Great heavens, Holmes!" I cried. "How utterly amazing!"

"Were there risks in this plan? Very few, and, as it turned out, none that tripped him. But, oh, he will trip, and very soon, too. He will fall so very, very far. It will be a downfall quite as complete as that of his ugly a mentor. The answer to the theological question and the series of questions that quickly follow it will, I think, break his armour. Do you remember my telegram to His Holiness which I have shared with you? The true Cardinal Palombello would be able to discuss the point quite thoroughly. If I am right, despite all their concern for outward trappings, and the ingenuity of the scheme, Moriarty's minion will not be able to hold his own on so obscure a point of theology. All politeness will fade. His Holiness will confront this Palombello like a schoolboy. It will be made apparent that he is a false priest. My old friend the Pope is not such a poor detective in his own right,'" Holmes chuckled, "when it comes to certain matters within the range of his expertise.

"I suppose that some of this will eventually reach the public. In any event, I know that you are the very soul of discretion, after the harrowing events of the Reichenbach Falls and my own return in the matter that you have entitled 'The Empty House.' I would not dream of excluding you from the details of this unusual case, my dear fellow. And, now, if you would be so kind as to receive back your very useful copy of the Strand magazine, I will bestow upon you as a memento of the present case Stamford's excellent map of the streets of the *regio nove* of the Eternal City. And, could you please hand me that small volume lying upon the side table that deals with the poisons of the canaries?"

FINALE

"I have never known my friend to be in better form, & both mental and physical, than in the year '95. His increasing fame had brought with it an immense practice, and I should be guilty of an indiscretion if I were to hint at the identity of some of the illustrious clients who crossed our humble threshold in Baker Street. In this memorable year '95, a curious and incongruous succession of cases had engaged his attention, ranging from his famous investigation of the sudden death of Cardinal Tosca—an inquiry that was carried out by him at the express desire of His Holiness, the Pope— down to his arrest of Wilson, the notorious canary-trainer, which removed a plague spot from the East End of London." |

     — The Adventure of Black Peter.

SOME IRREGULAR, AND NOT ENTIRELY REVERENT, RUMINATIONS ON THE BASKERVILLE KNIGHTHOODS

By Kelvin I. Jones and Roger Johnson.

Roger: (who has noted in the proof copy of 'THE ANNOTATED HOUND OF THE BASKERVILLES' that I have - mistakenly? referred to Hugo as 'Sir Hugo'):

The original, wicked, Hugo Baskerville is never referred to in the novel as "Sir Hugo". It seems to have been the cinema that made him a knight or baronet, whereas the implication in the novel is that the baronetcy was created for a later Baskerville. (We're never told whether Hugo had legitimate children. Probably not, as I don't recall mention of a wife, so the manor presumably passed to a brother, or possibly a cousin, who may have been the first Baskerville baronet.)

Kelvin: Roger (humorously)...My excuse for the unearned knighthood is now abundantly clear to me...I had my head full of 'Sir Henry...' And Peter Cushing, of course!

Roger: The Baskerville title is a baronetcy, which, unlike a knighthood, is hereditary. Even more confusing, although the name implies that a baronet is a sort of mini-baron, ranking immediately below a baron on the social scale, he is not a peer of the realm. So, when Watson explains to Beryl Stapleton that he isn't Sir Henry Baskerville: "Only a humble commoner, but his friend," he's apparently unaware that Sir Henry himself is a commoner.

Henry Baskerville tells Holmes and Watson, "I don't know much of British life yet, for I have spent nearly all my time in the States and in Canada." Nearly all, which implies, I think, that he was born in England and may have spent his early childhood here. His father - the middle brother, whose name we aren't told - died young, but we don't know where or how old Henry was at that time. The father may have taken his wife and child out to North America, to start a new life there; Sir Charles spent time in

South Africa, and the third brother, Rodger, "made England too hot to hold him, fled to Central America, and died there in 1876 of yellow fever." Then again, perhaps Henry's mother was American or Canadian; if her husband died when Henry was a very young child, she may have taken him with her, back to her own homeland. At any rate, there's no indication at all that Henry Baskerville wasn't a British citizen, though he may have held dual nationality. If Sir Henry did marry Beryl Stapleton, she would become Lady Baskerville. There's a good article in the Encyclopaedia Britannica online. The main part of it reads:

'Baronet, British hereditary dignity, first created by King James I of England in May 1611. The baronetage is not part of the peerage, nor is it an order of knighthood. A baronet ranks below barons but above all knights except, in England, Knights of the Garter and, in Scotland, Knights of the Garter and of the Thistle. In England and Ireland, a baronetcy is inherited by the male heir, but in Scotland ladies may succeed to certain baronetcies where it has been specified at the time of their creation.'

James I, desperate for funds as were all the Stuarts, decided to institute by letters patent "a new dignitie between Barons and Knights." Because the money was ostensibly for support of the troops in Ulster, candidates for the baronetage were required to pay the king £1,095 (the sum required to maintain 30 soldiers for three years), but such requirements were soon abandoned. In 1619, a baronetage of Ireland was also established, and in 1624 James planned another creation in connection with the plantation of Nova Scotia. This was completed after his death by Charles I in 1625.

The baronets of Scotland (or of Nova Scotia) were required to pay a total of £2,000 (the amount required to support six colonists) and to pay a fee of £1,000 to Sir William Alexander (afterward Earl of Stirling), to whom the province had been granted in 1621. In return they received, as well as their title, 16,000 acres of land in Nova Scotia. The creation of baronets of Scotland and of England ceased with the union of those countries in 1707; thereafter, until 1800, the new baronetcies were those of Great Britain. No more Irish baronets were created after the Irish Act of Union in 1801. From 1801 all creations were of baronets of the United Kingdom.

Kelvin: Hadn't Cabell, the basis for Hugo, been referred to as 'Sir'? There seemed to be some doubt about that...but could Hugo have been a Sir in real life - yes, quite likely, if he had been a supporter of the monarchy AS CABELL HAD BEEN, before he renounced the King - thus earning him the disfavour of the inhabitants of Dartmoor!! So maybe my calling Hugo 'Sir' wasn't so stupid after all...

Hang on, I thought...

But why 'Sir Henry'? - surely, I reasoned, a knighthood; wasn't it in some period of British history, an hereditary honour? And why Sir Charles...?

Then I began to gather some evidence:

Persons who conferred knighthoods on behalf of the sovereign in the 19th century included the Chief Governors of Ireland. In Ireland, The Order of St Patrick was founded in 1783 by George III for the Kingdom of Ireland, and after the Acts of Union 1800 continued for Irish peers in the United Kingdom of Great Britain and Ireland. After the Irish Free State's secession in 1922, only members of the royal family were appointed to the order, the last being in 1936.

If Sir Henry had lived for the major part of his life in Ireland and then emigrated to the USA, might this be the source of his knighthood?

The last surviving knight was Prince Henry, Duke of Gloucester, who died on 10 June 1974. Although dormant, the order technically still exists, and may be used as an award at any time. Queen Elizabeth II is the current sovereign of this order. KNIGHT is the same as a baronet in usage but is a title for life only. His wife will be 'Lady' plus "surname." The title of "Sir" is given to anyone awarded knighthood by the Queen, or a member of the royal family, acting in her stead. Knighthood can also be awarded for military service, or to anyone deemed a significant contributor to national life. Members of the clergy and foreign citizens who are awarded a knighthood, however, cannot use the title of "Sir." So that seems very clear to me.

If Sir Henry was an American citizen – which I believe he certainly was – he certainly could not have wandered around the Baskerville estate calling himself 'Sir Henry.' And neither would Barrymore have been entitled to address him thus. And neither, of course, would Watson or Holmes.

'In order to be granted knighthood, one must be dubbed as such by the Queen. The dubbing occurs during a ceremony, conducted publicly or in private, where the Queen awards knighthood using a sword and by presenting insignia of knighthood. When a clergy member is awarded knighthood, a sword is not used because it is not considered appropriate to the station of the clergy. Knighthood cannot be bought or solicited, and it does not imply military duty to the Queen. The female version of knighthood is known as damehood. The children of a knight or dame are not granted the title on virtue of their birth. Knights are required to earn the title through military honour, scientific achievement, civic achievement, or other invaluable contribution to the country or crown.' - (an amalgam here of various bits from the internet).

Roger, these points need more investigation

1. What EXACTLY had Sir Charles done to earn him a knighthood? Or was he referred to as SIR Charles because of the baronetcy.

2. Surely, Sir Henry cannot have used - legitimately, this title, on British soil, being a foreign (American) citizen. Why then call himself - 'Sir Henry'? What was going on here? Was Sir Henry a legitimate claimant or was he, in fact, yet another arbitrary imposter, like Stapleton?

3. And what about Beryl? If Beryl had married Sir Henry, would she have been known in Dartmoor as Dame Beryl Baskerville? Or simply Lady Baskerville? (See Roger's note, above.)

Roger: It occurs to me that, though there's no firm evidence, Hugo Baskerville, who recorded the story of the Hound in 1742 may well have been Sir Hugo. It's evident that he and his children, Rodger, John and

Elizabeth, lived on Dartmoor (see his admonition to his sons at the end of the manuscript), which suggests that he is the master of Baskerville Hall. He says at the beginning: "I come in a direct line from Hugo Baskerville." So, the estate passed from the original Hugo to a son (or, less likely, a daughter, whose husband adopted the Baskerville name; such a procedure was not unknown), but whether that child was born in wedlock is unknown. If the heir was a daughter or an illegitimate son, there could well have been provision for her or him to inherit the property, though only a legitimate son could have inherited a title, should we insist on giving the wicked father the honour of being Sir Hugo Baskerville, Bt.

However, I digress...

Unfortunately, we don't know when the baronetcy was conferred, or upon which particular Baskerville. Besides Sir Charles and Sir Henry, the only titled member of the family mentioned is "Sir William Baskerville, who was Chairman of Committees of the House of Commons under Pitt" - but we aren't told which Pitt. William Pitt the elder was Prime Minister from July 1766 to October 1768, but in August 1766, he was ennobled as the first Earl of Chatham. I suspect that Sir William Baskerville served under William Pitt the younger, Lord Chatham's second son, who didn't have a title. He was Prime Minister, successively of Great Britain, and then, of the United Kingdom, from December 1783 until his death at the age of 46, in January 1806.

That name "Rodger" always struck me as curious. There's no one in the canon called "Roger" with the usual spelling, and until the notorious Rodger Garrick-Steele came along with his wild conspiracy theory about the true authorship of The Hound, I'd never heard of anyone in real life who spelled his given name that way (the whole name appears to be made up, anyway).

I think it was Owen Dudley Edwards who drew what is undoubtedly the correct conclusion. 150 years ago, "Rodger" was a reasonably well = known surname in the Edinburgh area, though it seems to be very rare in England, and for some reason that particular spelling had become firmly stuck in ACD's mind. He used it again, you'll remember, for the forger Rodger Prescott in "The Three Garridebs".

Kelvin: Fair enough, Rodger; I find myself inclined to bow to your considerable erudition on the question of the knighthood of Sir Henry. I still remain curious though, about the knighthood of Sir Charles Baskerville. We know that he was well liked among Dartmoor residents for his philanthropic acts. And we know he was a businessman who was worth an extraordinary amount of money. We also know he was a bachelor. Yet, as the footnotes to my annotated edition clearly demonstrate, the exact nature of his relationship with Laura Lyons, the 'fallen woman' of the novel, is unclear. We know that Stapleton had enjoyed a sexual relationship with her. It was he

The sort of photograph that Dr Mortimer
and Sir Charles would have enjoyed examining
together at Baskerville Hall. A woman with the
anatomical shape termed steatopygia, a condition
in which the fatty acid composition of adipose tissue
 accumulates in an exaggerated way in the pelvic girdle.

who persuaded her to write the note which lured Sir Charles to his death. Had he also been having an intimate relationship with Laura? Was he a compulsive womaniser and had she been blackmailing him?

What were the precise sources of his vast income? We know that he spent a considerable time discussing with Dr Mortimer the physical assets of Hottentot women and their protuberant buttocks. They were obviously much preoccupied by steatopygia, a condition in which the fatty acid composition of adipose tissue accumulates in an exaggerated way in the pelvic girdle. This is more prominent in the subcutaneous tissue of the gluteal and femoral muscles. It was a predominant genetic characteristic in women, usually from African tribes.

It has been suggested by some archaeologists that this feature was once more widespread. Palaeolithic Venus figurines, often referred to as "Steatopygian Venus" figures, were first discovered by 19th Century archaeologists, from Europe to Asia, and these figures usually presented a remarkable development of the thighs. Even the prolongation of the labia minora have been used to support this theory. Whether these were intended to be lifelike, or perhaps even idealistic, is unclear, since they originate from a time prior to recorded history. Could it be that Mortimer, through his excavations on the Moor, had discovered several of the figurines? These figures, however, do not quite qualify as steatopygian, since they exhibit an angle of approximately 120 degrees between the back and the buttocks, while steatopygia is diagnosed by modern medical standards at an angle of about 90 degrees. However, the question remains: was the preoccupation shared by Mortimer and Sir Charles based on scholarly interest or mere prurience? And what exactly was the basis of Sir Charles' immense personal wealth and his knighthood? These are deep, dark waters, Watson.

Roger: You're determined to give Sir Charles Baskerville a knighthood, despite the clear statement in the novel that the family title is a baronetcy. In the last chapter, "A Retrospection", Holmes refers to Sir Charles four times as "the baronet". Throughout the novel, Sir Henry is referred to no fewer than 38 times as a "baronet". The words "knight" and "knighthood" are entirely absent.

Kelvin: Consider that a 'palpable hit,' Roger. You have clearly proven the case. Charles was entitled to use the appellation 'Sir' entirely because of the baronetcy. But what about my other, quite palpable and probably, entirely unreasonable, accusations about Charles?

Roger: You're also determined to give Sir Henry American citizenship. If he had any but British nationality, which I doubt, then why not Canadian? He did say that he'd spent "nearly all my time in the States and in Canada", but he didn't say how that time was divided between the two countries, and he was farming in Canada when he was informed of Sir Charles's death. Since 1919 Canadian citizens have been barred by their own government from accepting honours from the reigning monarch (about 20 years ago) there was a bit of a diplomatic row because two Canadians living in the UK had been knighted; apparently those responsible hadn't been aware of their nationality. However, before 1919 there was no such rule, so if young Henry Baskerville was a Canadian citizen there'd have been no obstacle to his inheriting the title.

(The American actor-director Christopher Guest - of This Is Spinal Tap, and husband of Jamie Lee Curtis - is the fifth Baron Haden-Guest of Saling, in the County of Essex. He was one of the last hereditary peers to sit in the House of Lords by right, before Tony Blair's reformation of the House took effect. However, he has dual American and British citizenship, as Sir Henry Baskerville may have done.)

Kelvin: Fair enough. So, because Henry had dual nationality, he was therefore entitled to be referred to as 'Sir Henry.' Now I see the error of my thinking....

Roger: Your mention of the now dormant Order of St Patrick reminds me that there is one hereditary title of knight in Ireland. Originally three were created by Edward III: the White Knight, the Black Knight (the Knight of Glin) and the Green Knight (the Knight of Kerry). The last White Knight died in the 19th century, and the last Knight of Glin in 2011, but the

24th Knight of Kerry is alive and well. As the Knight of Kerry he would be addressed as "Knight", but he's also, like Sir Charles and Sir Henry Baskerville, a baronet, so he's more usually known as Sir Adrian Fitzgerald.

Kelvin: And what about this business of Sir Charles, Mortimer and the Hottentot women?

Roger: I really do think that you're unjustifiably maligning Dr Mortimer and Sir Charles Baskerville. Yes, the good doctor does say: "... many a charming evening we have spent together discussing the comparative anatomy of the Bushman and the Hottentot," but he makes it quite clear that he and Sir Charles shared "a community of interests in science". Your image of the two men slavering lasciviously over descriptions of steatopygous Saan and Khoikoi women has no basis in the characters as depicted in the novel.

Kelvin: Roger, I think my point may be nevertheless justifiable. Mortimer says they spent 'many a charming evening' discussing the comparative anatomy of the two racial types. Why would they be doing this repeatedly, if not for 'lascivious' reasons, as you eloquently put it? And what about that business of Laura Lyons? Why was Barrymore so secretive about mentioning (or not mentioning) to the coroner the note and the business of the clandestine meeting, between Charles and Laura, if not to conceal *some possible indiscretion?* Moreover, why was Laura so reluctant to tell Watson the whole story of their relationship when he went to see her?

And one more point, regarding the activities of Mortimer. What was he doing digging up human remains on the Moor when we know for a fact *that no human skull has ever been found on Dartmoor?* Did he not know that the Bronze Age people practised cremation rather than inhumation? Whose remains was he actually digging up? When Mortimer first visits Holmes, you will recall he says to him:

'I had hardly expected so dolichocephalic a skull or such well-marked supra-orbital development. Would you have any objection to my running my finger along your parietal fissure? A cast of your skull, sir, until the original is available, would be an ornament to any anthropological museum. It is not my intention to be fulsome, but I confess that I covet your skull.'

What on earth did he mean by this? Most clearly, he was a collector of skulls. But just how did he obtain them? I note a recent bulletin from the BBC, which comments:

'Australian Aborigines have long campaigned for the repatriation of human remains held in British museums and universities. They regard such collections as an affront to their customs and spiritual way of life. The Tasmanian materials were largely collected in the 19th Century by George Augustus Robinson who had been contracted by the colonial government of the day to clear lands by force for European settlers. On his death, the remains were passed into the possession of other individuals and eventually deposited in UK institutions, and then gradually brought under the keeping of the Natural History Museum. They will now be given, through the Australian government, to the Tasmanian Aboriginal Centre (TAC), which has been in dispute over the matter for more than 20 years.' During Robinson's time in Tasmania and Victoria, he collected many objects and artworks from the aboriginal communities. After his death, his widow Rose sold the items to many museums. These included many human remains. The British Museum had 138 items relating to Robinson's time in Australia, including aboriginal artefacts, prints and drawings. Joseph Barnard Davis acquired many from Robinson's widow in the 1860s, and it may be through his activities that objects subsequently found their way into other collections, for example at the British Museum.'

I decided therefore to research this whole area of the Victorian gentleman/archaeologist's fascination with the collection of human remains from disadvantaged people, and came up with some pretty disturbing data. In May, 1901, an article appeared in the Yarmouth Advertiser and Gazette, entitled 'Alleged Traffic in Pauper Corpses—How the Medical Schools are Supplied—The Shadow of a Scandal'. It recorded that, although a pauper named Frank Hyde aged fifty had died in Yarmouth workhouse on 11 April 1901, his body was missing from the local cemetery. The case caused a public outcry because the workhouse death register stated that Hyde had been "buried by friends" in the parish five days after he had died. An editorial alleged that "the body was sent to Cambridge for dissection" instead, and that the workhouse Master's clerk profited 15 shillings from the cadaver's sale.

Following continued bad publicity, the visiting committee of Yarmouth Union investigated the allegations. They discovered that between 1880 and 1901 '26 bodies' had been sold for dissection and dismemberment under the terms of the Anatomy Act (1832) to the Cambridge anatomical teaching school situated at Downing College. The Master's clerk staged a false funeral each time a pauper died in his care. He arranged it so that 'coffins were buried containing sand or sawdust or other ingredients but the body of the person, whose name appeared on the outside of each coffin, never reached the grave.' This was Hyde's fate too. Like many paupers who died in the care of Poor Law authorities in the nineteenth century, Hyde's friends and relatives lacked resources to fund his funeral expenses. Consequently, he underwent the ignominy of a pauper burial, but not in Yarmouth. His body was conveyed on the Great Eastern railway in a "death-box" to Cambridge anatomical teaching school. Following preservation, which took around four months, the cadaver was dissected and dismembered. It was not then interred until eleven months after death in St Benedict's parish graveyard within Mill Road cemetery, Cambridge, on 8 March 1902.

So then, Roger, it seems that Dr Mortimer probably had a great deal to discuss regarding the 'comparative anatomy' of the Hottentots and the Bushmen. Was this what Mortimer was referring to when he talked about 'the community of interests in science?'...I rest my case...

Roger: (sighs...To himself:) When will he ever stop theorising?

THE CONSULTING DETECTIVE AND THE LITERARY AGENT: The Untold Tale

by Barbara Rusch

In my relentless pursuit of the elusive ephemeral documents and unconventional artifacts relating to the era of "a certain gracious lady" and an "illustrious client," in 2012 I became the successful bidder on the intriguing contents of a cardboard box. On the lid is printed in ink, "Lady Conan Doyle, Windlesham, Crowborough," the home in East Sussex where ACD drew his final breath in 1930. The box is filled with – no, not a pair of mismatched human ears – but a collection of his wife's delicate undergarments. The provenance is indisputable, a white name tag stitched in red thread identifying the owner of the personal items in question. You may choose to scoff and snicker, and at first blush this drawerful of drawers appeared to be nothing more than a random assortment of frilly furbelows of silk and lace. But inside, wedged between the pantalets and the petticoats, previously undiscovered, were papers which initially appeared to be a kind of backing or stiffener, but upon closer inspection proved to be a folded manuscript of incalculable value. Herein hangs a tale for which the world may not yet be prepared, but with which it will nonetheless now be presented, yielding a treasure trove of secrets neither its original owner nor the British auction house from which I purchased it could have predicted. I have transcribed the poignant narrative it contains, penned in a familiar, neat, round hand, upon which no other eyes until this moment have fallen, and am pleased to share them with all those who, like me, possess an abiding admiration for three great men of our acquaintance. This is Conan Doyle's statement.

****

It was a raw, blustery day in November of the year 1894, and those few brave souls I passed in the roadway had their coats buttoned up and their heads bent low against the onslaught of the first fierce blast of the season. The last withered leaves clung defiantly to the great oak-tree outside 221B Baker Street, as if their obstinacy could somehow forestall the inevitability of Nature's death sentence. I paused before ringing the bell, debating silently whether I should proceed or would come to regret the decision to embark upon this painful journey. As I lifted my eyes, I could see Sherlock Holmes gazing down from the bow window, as he often did in anticipation of a client who hesitated upon his doorstep before making the inevitable decision to enter. Mrs. Hudson ushered me up those storied seventeen steps to the cluttered sitting room, where newspaper clippings and pots of glue littered the floor and coated several of the arm-chairs. Both Holmes and Watson looked puzzled as to my identity under my greatcoat and slouch hat.

"Why, it's our old friend and literary agent, Conan Doyle," exclaimed Watson, once I had unravelled myself from these latter-day mummy's wrappings. "I thought I recognized those elegant mustachios peeping out from beneath your muffler. Delighted to see you, Doctor. Please excuse the disorder. Allow me to find a more advantageous spot for these papers. Holmes is assembling some additional pages to insert into his index."

I was well aware that the great consulting detective had made an avocation of filing as complete a dossier as may be imagined clipped from the agony columns of the various London newspapers and journals. Over the years there was hardly a missing person or a mislaid possession of which he was unaware. It seemed as though everyone was searching for something – or someone – and Holmes had been tasked with singlehandedly monitoring this enormous national lost and found department. Moreover, he had developed his own peculiar system of docketing all manner of people and events, most especially ones relating to crimes and those who perpetrated them. These he meticulously pasted into the bulging scrapbooks he referred to affectionately as "good old index," which sat conspicuously on the topmost shelf of the sitting room. From this promontory, his ponderous commonplace books came to represent as comprehensive a repository of knowledge on the subject of the celebrated and notorious as one is likely to encounter outside a headline in The Times or a glass display case at New Scotland Yard's Black Museum.

Gathering a jumbled armful of the aforementioned newspaper cuttings that had been draped over an arm-chair, Watson deposited them in a pile on a nearby occasional table in the centre of the room, upon which a framed image of a handsome lady, elegantly coiffed and fashionably attired, whom I recognized immediately as the celebrated contralto Irene Adler, took pride of place. As he proceeded to awkwardly set down the bundle of scraps, the photograph inadvertently toppled over. Holmes, as upset as the picture, leaped to his feet and darted across the room. Using his coat sleeve, he ceremoniously brushed away remnants of dust and debris which as a consequence had found their way onto the glass. His lips drawn into a taut, thin line, his voice cracking with an emotion he could scarcely contain, he softly admonished, "Do take care, Watson."

"My most sincere apologies, Holmes. I assure you it was quite unintentional," replied his flustered colleague in a conciliatory tone, abandoning the papers altogether. "There we are. Do make yourself at home, Doctor Doyle." Hoping to set things right in more than one sense, and in an effort to place himself out of Holmes's line of vision and divert attention from the unfortunate turn the visit had taken, Watson sat down gingerly on a settee at a safe distance from his somewhat peevish companion. His arm stretched languidly across the back of his chair, he assumed a studied, if less than convincing, air of breezy nonchalance. I in turn settled into the recently vacated and slightly worn seat he had indicated.

"Now then, Doctor, as I have often told you," said Watson, whose nerves appeared quite as frayed as the furniture, and understandably eager to steer the conversation onto a more neutral path and restore a sense of tranquillity to the scene, "I am everlastingly in your debt in my trifling attempts to bring before the public the adventures of our sedulous sleuth, who largely on your account has come to enjoy a certain celebrity." I could not help but feel that at least a modicum of that flattering observation was proffered with a view to being reinstated into his friend's good graces, while I was thrust into the unenviable position of buffer between the fractious fellow lodgers.

"And I congratulate you," he added, "on becoming something of a literary lion in your own right, what with your tales of horror and historical romance. Your recent endeavours have met with nothing short of unanimous acclaim within our narrow sphere, and I have it on good authority that they have attracted a large and enthusiastic readership."

"I fear my inconsequential scribblings are no more than competent at best," I replied, "though I do pride myself on my modest forays into the age of chivalry. But I thank you most sincerely for your generous endorsement, most especially as I confess to taking as my inspiration your thrilling accounts of Holmes's heroic exploits. Perhaps you have surmised that my gallant medieval knights are modelled after our friend here, though I fear they pale by comparison with the original."

"The possibility had certainly occurred to me," Watson chuckled. "But I have something of a discriminating eye for such things, and am prepared to prophesy without the slightest hesitation that you will come to enjoy unparalleled success as a prestigious and prolific author in your own right. Indeed, your considerable talents have not been misdirected. I foresee an illustrious career ahead of you."

I own to feeling a slight swelling of pride within my bosom. "Coming from you, Doctor Watson, such profuse accolades are indeed gratifying," Truth be told, his encomium was nothing short of music to my ears and went some way toward buoying my spirits.

"No doubt these are matters of surpassing interest," grumbled Holmes, growing clearly impatient at all this polite palaver. "But I sense that there is something other than an exchange of pleasantries which brings you to our humble lodgings in the teeth of such inclement weather. Perhaps I may be of service to you in some small way?"

"Well, for one, Holmes, I have come to welcome you back, not just to London, but from the brink of death, having learned of your near fatal encounter at the precipice of that fearsome cataract."

"Ah yes, that 'seething cauldron,' or some such nonsense, as Watson so euphemistically phrased it. I suppose he cannot do otherwise," he grimaced. "It is his natural inclination to indulge in poetic excess, the results of which you may judge for yourself in his slightly lurid tales. But then, as our literary agent, you are all too familiar with his flair for the dramatic," he sniffed, casting an accusatory glance at the culpable chronicler he was known to refer to as his "Boswell" when in a more magnanimous disposition. Looking somewhat abashed, that kind-hearted gentleman, having recovered his good humour, turned to me with a mischievous wink.

"Not nearly so poetical from inside it, I assure you," muttered Holmes with a rueful sigh, returning to the subject of the Reichenbach Falls, that terrible chasm where he had come so near to meeting his demise in that deathly struggle with the evil Professor Moriarty. "My subsequent travels are, to my mind, of far greater interest," he observed, almost as an afterthought. "Perhaps one day I shall document them myself, without benefit of lyrical embellishment. Now that would be poetic justice!" he exclaimed triumphantly, glaring once again at his undeservedly maltreated biographer, as if to put him on formal notice. "Nevertheless, many thanks, Doyle. It is indeed good to be back."

"No doubt we shall be reading of both your adventures and misadventures when your memoirs are released, and I hope to have the honour of assisting in their publication. But," I hastened to add, "once again you are correct, Holmes. I see very little escapes you. There was a matter on which I wished to confer with you."

"Watson," said Holmes, "throw another lump or two of coal onto the grate and for heaven's sake, ring Mrs. Hudson for some tea, and perhaps something bracing besides, to help fortify the good doctor's constitution, and perhaps his spirits, for unless I am very much mistaken, he is sorely in need of a bit of medicinal buttressing."

And indeed, I was feeling rather peaked, and found myself shivering uncontrollably. Glad to warm myself by the fire, which by now was crackling and blazing cheerily away, and dispensing with the tea altogether,

I took a grateful draught of the brandy offered to me and attempted to gather my thoughts.

"And now, Doctor," resumed Holmes, "how may I assist you?"

"I well know," I began haltingly, a slight quaver in my voice, "that you are no Father Confessor. Nor is 221B a confessional, though I am aware it has served as one on occasion. And yet my heart is heavy and I know of nowhere else to turn in my desperation and despair. As my medical colleague here so eloquently expressed it when we all believed you to be lying lifeless at the bottom of that awful abyss, you are also 'the best and the wisest man whom I have ever known,' with the uncanny facility to see into the darkest recesses of the human soul. I therefore turn to you and solicit your best counsel."

"But what could possibly be the cause of such affliction?"

"A terrible injustice," I responded.

"Perpetrated by whom?" inquired Holmes, his expression intent, his eyes gleaming like a cat's, his long fingers steepled beneath his chin in anticipation.

"By me."

"And the crime?"

"A most heinous one, to which Dante would have consigned the miscreant to the depths of the Inferno – a sin for which I shall be equally condemned – that of a son against his own father."

Watson, leaning forward in keen expectation, looked utterly mystified, and the expression on Holmes's face was one of incredulity at this startling confession. "I am all attention. Pray proceed."

Propping myself up on the horsehair cushions, I sighed deeply and commenced my painful narrative.

"My story is soon told," I began hesitantly. "You may know that just over a year ago my father passed beyond the veil."

"I learned of your sad bereavement some months later, upon my arrival in France, and was sorry indeed to hear it. I offer you my condolences, my friend. I admired Charles Altamont Doyle a great deal. He was a man of enormous heart and a gifted artist besides. Naturally I was indebted to him for his drawings in an early edition of the minor adventure which Watson embellished with the title A Study in Scarlet."

"Yes," I murmured softly, "it would seem that sufficient time has elapsed to blunt my grief, and yet each day brings with it fresh sorrow which I have brought upon myself. My father was a man of sensitive genius, ill-suited to the realities of this world. His mind was on strange moonlight effects, done with extraordinary skill in water colours. He had a charm of manner and a courtesy of bearing which I have seldom seen equalled. But he was in many ways a tormented creature and his life was blighted in consequence of underdeveloped gifts and unfulfilled dreams. After a promising early career as a draughtsman, he became subject to excruciating headaches, plunging him into frequent bouts of deep depression. A weakness for drink, which I have made a concerted effort to conceal, was accompanied by hallucinatory episodes, and his declining years were spent confined to a series of asylums within whose bleak corridors I rarely called upon him. I did little to ease the burdens he bore, nor was I in any way attentive to his needs. Truth be told, I could summon up no great sympathy either for him or for the desperate situation in which he found himself. My resentment at having to fend for myself and see to the demands of my family as I struggled through medical school fuelled our estrangement and hardened my resolve. We referred to his condition as the 'dreadful secret.' I am ashamed to confess that my thoughts were solely for the disadvantage which his condition placed upon me and not for his anguish nor the deplorable manner in which I had abandoned him to his lonely fate. Perhaps I harboured a fear that his infirmities might prove hereditary, for I am all too aware that such unfortunate predispositions may be passed down from one generation to the next."

At this point in my lachrymose lament I paused to take another long draught of the brandy, then pressed on. "Ultimately, the breach brought on by my disreputable conduct became so vast as to be irreconcilable. My father's malady manifested in a morbid fascination with death, and I imagine the end must have been something of a consolation for him. I pray he has at last found peace. But now I am the tormented one, haunted by a calculated indifference and consumed with a remorse from which I can find no respite. What a loathsome creature I am. How could I have allowed him to languish in that desolate place, without a devoted son to bring solace to his wounded spirit and tortured soul? Now his passing, forlorn and un mourned, weighs heavily upon my conscience, and the 'dreadful secret' has become my own shame and despair. I cannot help but reproach myself, and struggle within the depths of a pit of regret and contrition from which there is no escape."

By the conclusion of my plaintive saga, I had quite collapsed into convulsive sobs, a shattered wreck, burying my face in my hands. "Steady, my dear fellow," said Holmes, reaching across and gripping me by the arm in a well-intentioned, if ineffectual, effort to console me. "Try to pull yourself together, man." No doubt he feared I had taken leave of my senses, and at that moment I allow to sharing his concerns. "Watson, some more brandy."

With the amiable doctor ministering to my needs, I gradually regained control of my trembling limbs, along with some semblance of composure. Holmes, meanwhile, grew contemplative, gazing pensively into the fire, his old briar pipe clenched between his lips, swirling eddies of blue smoke partially obscuring his features. His normally piercing grey eyes assumed a far-away look, as if lost in distant reverie. After a few moments, he broke the silence that had descended upon the sitting room, while without, the gale shook furiously at the window-pane like a prisoner rattling the bars of his cell, the curtains drawn in defiance against the inexorable forces of nature.

"I appreciate your candour in these matters, Doctor – in addition to your feelings of self-recrimination," he began in grim and deliberate reflection. "We are none of us blameless with respect to a wayward father. Mine, you may know, was a country squire who boasted a naturally genial manner, but was transformed into an odious brute when in his cups. His vicious ways drove me at a tender age from the only home I had ever known. But that was as nothing when set against the terrible cruelty he inflicted upon my mother, beaten up and broken down, and my university days came to an abrupt end when I was compelled to return to intercede on her behalf, convinced that her life was imperilled. I have prevailed upon Watson to withhold these distressing details from his published narratives. Public exposure of the true facts might prove something of an inconvenience to me and particularly incommodious to my brother Mycroft in his sensitive position in the Foreign Office. The fate that befell the old blackguard does not bear close scrutiny, though I am prepared to affirm that the justice meted out to him in the end was a righteous one and not likely to weigh very heavily upon my conscience. Can you wonder, then, at my reticence on the subject of my forebears? And yet, the brutality I witnessed in those tender years was no doubt a deciding factor in my choice of métier. Watson will tell you that I am especially offended by the outrages committed by violent men upon ill-used, if weak-willed, women, whether wives or daughters, whose molesters I endeavour to run to ground. I do not suffer the Grimesby Roylotts or Jack Stapletons of this world gladly, though I own that in holding them to account for their crimes I am in some small measure seeking justice for the suffering of a dear mother at the hands of an implacable father."

You may only wonder at the effect this unexpected confession had upon my already agitated mind. No doubt the astonishment etched on my face registered it all. For this inscrutable, self-contained and intensely private man to have divulged to me the previously undisclosed secrets of his troubled parentage was at once disconcerting and humbling. Moreover, these unhappy revelations provided incontrovertible evidence that, despite his well-known distaste for intimacy, Sherlock Holmes is as far from the cold, calculating machine Watson has portrayed him as may be imagined. To the contrary, it was becoming abundantly clear that here was a fellow of unimpeachable integrity, whose strength of character concealed a very private heartache, one possessed of a profound inner life from which he drew his unshakeable moral integrity and an unwavering commitment to justice. I suddenly grasped as I never could before that the ill-fortune which attended his youth had cast an indelible shadow over him, in consequence whereof that part of his solitary nature so averse to modifying his passions had been sacrificed to a resolute austerity. The epiphany brought me ever closer to the humanity of the man behind the myth.

"I was unaware you lay claim to this dark past, Holmes," I declared in astonishment.

"I have confided in you the blackest days of my youth as an act of faith, by way of assuring you that your confidence in me has not been misplaced. You may count on me to treat it with the utmost discretion and counsel you in this matter with the benefit of my own experience. And my advice to you is this: we cannot turn back the hands of time, Doyle. But there is one thing we can do. Pay tribute to an honourable, if failed, father. Sing his praises, take pride in his many excellent attributes and find the means to assimilate them into your own endeavours. Think of it as a kind of spiritual collaboration, if you will. Above all, you must find it in your heart to forgive him – and yourself."

I was quite overwhelmed with Holmes's insight and sage advice, and could feel my melancholy perceptibly lifting away like dark clouds dispersing after a storm. As if to confirm this restored sense of tranquillity, the howling beyond the window-pane had suddenly ceased. "My friend, I cannot thank you enough for your kind ministrations and judicious admonitions, and pledge on my oath to be guided by them. What you have done today is as great a service as any of the crimes you have solved and clients to whose aid you have come. Please accept my most sincere gratitude. I shall be forever in your debt." As always, Watson conveyed it best in a rather more generous appraisal of his boon companion, for on that day "I caught a glimpse of a great heart as well as of a great brain."

****

In the years following that pivotal moment in the sitting room of 221B I have made every effort to keep the promise I made to Holmes and to myself. As frequently befalls us in life, the hand of fate pointed irrevocably toward my destiny. Though my talents do not lie with brush or paint, I have indeed incorporated my father's passions and convictions into my own work. To that end, the monstrous prehistoric beasts and flying creatures of my adventure tale The Lost World took as their inspiration his sketches of enormous and menacing woodland creatures in pursuit of terrified and delicate waifs. Given his and my Uncle Dicky's predilection for fairies, it is more than probable that my own obsession with elementals is at least in part some perverse biological imperative. Fairies in the blood are liable to take the strangest forms. I would be hesitant to confess to it publicly, but if I am being absolutely truthful, as I feel compelled to do in this confidential memoir, I concede that the photographs of the Cottingley fairies, in whose authenticity I professed an abiding conviction, might well have been no more than an elaborate hoax. Nevertheless, upon reflection, the incident afforded me the opportunity to redeem my father's memory, to give meaning to his life and the hallucinatory world he inhabited – and to assuage my guilt. In 1924 I organized an exhibition of some fifty of his beautiful, haunting and disturbing paintings which was well received by critics and public alike. My affiliation with the spiritualist movement, which many attribute to the loss of my son Kingsley following the Great War, was sparked decades earlier in a vain attempt to re-establish a connection on another plane with my dear father. Much of my life, it seems, has been spent honouring the fourth commandment and perpetuating the legacy of Charles Altamont Doyle.

***

Over the next two decades, the relations I enjoyed with Sherlock Holmes had been pleasant and fruitful, both in a professional and a personal capacity, and I take some pride in the services I provided to both him and Dr. Watson as the literary agent for the extraordinary accounts of their many adventures together. I had not enjoyed the favour of a communication from Holmes for the two years prior to the Great War. Unpredictable to the point of eccentricity, he was liable to vanish as thoroughly as the elusive Houdini, my erstwhile friend and sometime rival, for years at a time when in pursuit of some murderous secret society or while being pursued by one himself, so I was not unduly concerned. After all, he had disappeared into thin air following his harrowing escape at the Reichenbach, so we had grown quite accustomed to his prolonged and inexplicable absences.

And yet, from time to time a nagging doubt as to his well-being overcame me, and I toyed with the idea of placing an advertisement in the agony column of the Times in an effort to reassure myself of his continued existence. At one point I had gone so far as to compose the notice, which read, in part:

Seeking the whereabouts of an exceedingly angular gentleman, somewhat above six feet in height, of austere demeanour and ascetic features - thin of hair and of lip, prominent of proboscis, of peculiarly penetrating eye and of pronounced eccentricities. Neatly dressed and scrupulously clean. Smokes shag tobacco. Has been known to carry a magnifying glass on his person with which he at a moment's notice might fall to the ground to examine the mud on the underside of the shoes of passers-by or the elbows of young women. The sum of £25 will be paid to anyone with information. Apply to the undersigned.

The irony did not escape me that searching the agony columns for the very man whose métier it was to search agony columns struck me as patently absurd, and upon further consideration I dismissed the notion out of hand.

As fate would have it, Holmes was neither mislaid property nor a missing person, and my worst fears were allayed late one afternoon in October of 1914, when he suddenly arrived, quite unannounced, on my doorstep at Windlesham, in Sussex, where I had made my home for some seven years past. Though his hair was noticeably flecked with grey, by all accounts he appeared hale and hearty, if discernibly more gaunt, his step firm, his bearing as erect and dignified as ever. His eyes retained their keen intensity, his senses were sharpened, and he seemed possessed of a surfeit of vigour. He fairly radiated purpose and vitality, his face aglow with what might best be described as triumphant exaltation. Though advancing in years, it was clear he was still at the height of his powers.

"I do hope I'm not intruding, Arthur," he said.

"You are most cordially welcome here. Delighted to see you, Sherlock," I assured him, gripping his hand until I nearly shook it off. "The pleasure is all the greater for being so unexpected. You honour us all at Windlesham with your presence. How often have I thought of you and wondered when I should be privileged to see you again. But to what great good fortune am I indebted for your attendance? And where the devil have you been, if I may be presumptuous enough to enquire?'

"A moment, Arthur, if you please. Allow me to explain."

"Ah, forgive me. I am derelict in my duties as host. I have neither taken your hat nor offered you anything by way of libation before subjecting you to this unpardonable inquisition. I fear my curiosity has got the better of me. A cheery fire and a glass of port will soon chase the chill from your bones. Let us adjourn to my library."

Holmes followed me into what I am pleased to refer to as my sanctum sanctorum, familiar yet notable in its own modest way, a snug, little, oak-panelled sanctuary lined with shelves overflowing with my most cherished volumes, culled over a lifetime. Just walking through that magic door is for me like entering an enchanted land of fantasy and imagination. Here is the jewel-case for my most precious possessions, within whose walls dwell the profound observations of the greatest philosophers, the critical assessments of the foremost chroniclers of history, and the ingenuity of the most spellbinding storytellers the world has known. Gazing round that chamber never fails to fill me with awe and serve as inspiration all at once – evidence of the indelible mark these forward thinkers and peerless savants have left on humanity. As I sit at my desk, pen in hand, I can almost feel their essence flowing through me as I attempt to emulate their genius to the limits of my ability.

I was gratified that Holmes appeared to appreciate the depth and diversity of the collection, as he took several minutes to peruse the shelves, remarking on a title here and an author there which particularly peaked his interest, stopping to examine the contents of one or two more closely.

"Do make yourself comfortable upon the old green settee," said I, once the inspection of the more salient tomes had concluded to his apparent satisfaction. I motioned him to the faded arm-chair before the fireplace, which has long been my favourite. On the wall above hung – and still does – a gilt-framed lithograph of the old Queen as she appeared on the occasion of her Diamond Jubilee. Though she had passed on to her just reward thirteen years before, I have been loath to remove her – either from my wall or from my heart. Her presence brings to mind the glorious age of a reign which will never be surpassed. For me, Victoria will ever remain the centrepiece of an Empire built to last. Truth be told, her image fondly recalls my own glory days as a callow youth with a head full of dreams and a taste for adventure, those early years aboard an Arctic whaler and as a struggling ophthalmologist, as I groped about for my true calling. Somehow I cannot bring myself to replace her portrait with that of her descendants, so there it has remained – her kindly countenance gazing benignly down upon me. In some way I find difficult to define, when the door closes behind me in that mystical chamber, time stands still – and it is always 1897. But my feeble act of fealty pales by comparison with that of her most loyal subject, whose own wall, irreparably bullet-pocked with Her Majesty's cipher, proclaims his undying devotion. When it comes to panache, Sherlock Holmes is ever the master.

Darkness was closing in fast, though I was reluctant to switch on the electric light. I am inordinately fond of moments of quiet reflection spent in rooms illuminated solely by firelight. Now, as the coals sizzled and sputtered in the grate, the flickering flames cast eerie shadows over the great detective's distinctive features, throwing his brooding eyes, aquiline nose and square-cut jaw into bold relief. The entire mise en scène was more than suggestive of one of Sidney Paget's charming drawings in The Strand Magazine, Holmes and Watson seated on either side of the fire at 221B Baker

Street, the image, deftly drawn in shades of grey, gradually fading into obscurity along the edges. As we nestled in, two glasses of ruby-tinted port glinting in the warm glow of the hearth, Holmes wasted no time in declaring the true purpose of his visit.

"Arthur," he began, "I am not unmindful that my absence has excited considerable speculation. The truth is, when it became clear that a sinister plot was afoot, I was called upon to undertake the most perilous mission of my career. For these two years past I have assumed the identity of an Irish-American agent in a life-or-death struggle against a ruthless and diabolical adversary. The very survival of the Empire might well have depended upon a successful outcome."

"You are a faithful friend, Sherlock, but a relentless foe. So you return to us the conquering hero, your brow once again wreathed in laurel," I exclaimed in all sincerity. "I congratulate you on vanquishing our enemies. You do us proud, sir – our champion – and a benefactor to mankind."

"Well, that remains to be seen," he shrugged in his singularly self-assured, yet understated, fashion. "I merely did what little I could. I leave the rest to others."

"Nevertheless," I insisted, "there's not an officer in all the King's regiments, from the newly-joined subaltern even to Field-Marshal Kitchener himself, who wouldn't be glad to shake you by the hand." To further punctuate the point, I rose and proffered him a mischievous, though by no means parodical, salute.

"Thank you. You are most kind," said Holmes, genuinely moved by my effusive praise. "The stars stand guard in the heavens, and in our own small way we are privileged to serve alongside them."

"And what of Dr. Watson?" I enquired. "Is he cognizant of your most recent triumph?"

"Indeed, he had a not insignificant role to play in it," Holmes conceded, "and at its conclusion we enjoyed a moment of quiet reflection as we stood upon the terrace of the drafty, old pile where the dénouement of this little drama was enacted. I will share with you now what I told him then – that, for better or for worse, the world is about to be irretrievably altered. We are embarking upon a new era in the history of civilization, one in which our lives will never be the same again."

"Be that as it may," I replied, "there remains one immutable truth of which I am certain. There will always be an England – and there will always be Sherlock Holmes. They are as inextricably bound and as essential to life as the air we breathe."

Leaning in, Holmes clasped me by the shoulder. "We shall see, Doyle," was his enigmatic response, a sad, little smile playing about his lips. "We shall see."

Clearing his throat, for his voice had become thick with emotion, he resumed his captivating narrative. "For the duration of this, my most challenging campaign, I was obliged to adopt a pseudonym."

"Ah, a mystery moniker, is it?' I chuckled, bemused and intrigued. "And by what name may I now have the pleasure of addressing you?"

"Altamont," replied Holmes, a sly twinkle in his eye.

"My father's name?" I managed to choke out in a barely audible whisper. I need hardly express the depth of my astonishment at that moment, as I suddenly felt all the air rush from my lungs and was left gasping for breath. I stared at him in utter bewilderment, though I should not have been entirely taken by surprise. I have learned over the years that while nothing about Holmes is entirely unanticipated, everything he says and does comes as something of a jolt to the system. And yet, as if in defiance of all expectation, at that moment I confess to being at a complete loss as to his meaning. As is his custom, he soon offered up a cogent explanation.

"Years ago I counselled you to pay homage to that fine man and worthy patriarch. What I refrained from disclosing, however, was that he and I had developed a fast friendship. He professed an abiding admiration for what he referred to – in somewhat excessive tribute – as my 'valiant efforts to seek justice in a cruel world,' and in an act of emulation, his renderings of me in A Study in Scarlet more closely resembled his own person. He may have envied me the freedom I enjoyed to follow my chosen path while he was constrained from fulfilling a nobler destiny by reason of ill health and psychological impairment. He took me into his confidence, freely acknowledging his many failings and regrets, despite which, I assure you, I returned his esteem." Holmes sipped at his port and sighed in wistful reminiscence. "In his own peculiar fashion he was a fellow of unsurpassed wisdom," adding, with only the slightest hesitation, "and the kind, gentle father for whom I longed."

His words hung in the air for a long moment. When my astonishment prevented me from immediately rejoining, he hastened to avert any further offence his admission might unintentionally have inflicted upon my sensibilities. "My most unequivocal apologies to have taken you unawares, Doyle, though I beg you to be in no way discomfited. Charles implored me to keep the nature of our relations from you in order to spare you any further pain. Now I have reciprocated his veneration, and in my own way have sought to keep his memory green." In truth, I found his declamation as heartening as it was startling. Here, it seemed, was a man who revered my father no less than I, one equally dedicated to honouring his legacy.

How could I do otherwise than accept the putative apology he proffered, the more so when he prevailed upon me (as he had on one previous occasion, with Watson's indulgence) to set down the record of his marvellous adventure, once sufficient time had elapsed to lay the facts of this vitally important case with as much circumspection as possible before the public. Thus my role as literary agent became somewhat enhanced, though, unlike my other attempts at authorship, this was no work of fiction. It is more than likely that Holmes entrusted its telling to me by virtue of my uniquely intimate association with it, though for this very reason we thought it prudent not to attach my name to the stirring events to which he affixed the fitting title His Last Bow. In reality, my contribution was little more than editorial in nature, so keen a grasp did he retain with regard to the minutest details of his unparalleled heroism. Thus Sherlock Holmes and I have each kept a pledge to my father, and I have perhaps in some small measure redeemed myself in his eyes. The bond we have forged has become indissoluble, my father's spirit having become the powerful force which unites us in brotherhood in the truest sense, indistinguishable pillars upon which a flourishing friendship has long been sustained. I cannot extol highly enough the exemplary virtues of one to whom I am indebted by the strongest ties of gratitude and affection.

I suspect my time on this earthly plane is growing short, and before long I shall permanently don the spiritual mantle whose principles and beliefs I have embraced so fervently in life. The hour of reclamation is at hand, as I prepare to be reunited with a father lost to me so long ago. For now, I shall safeguard the sensitive and confidential communications herein recorded, along with their concomitant – and possibly incendiary – repercussions, and will search for a clandestine and discreet niche in which to conceal them. No doubt the particulars will ultimately be divulged – to which I have no undue objection – and in any event by which time it will be beyond my power either to prevent their disclosure or to dispute their veracity. Should it come to pass that other eyes are cast upon these pages, I pray I will be judged with the same charity and compassion that Sherlock Holmes bestowed upon me and all those he deemed equally deserving, and be granted absolution. It may well be that this, my final testament, will one day serve as my epitaph.

A. Conan Doyle

June 6, 1930

****

So ends Conan Doyle's remarkable statement. As for me, what began as an acquisition of frivolous frippery has evolved into a chronicle of remorse, reconciliation and redemption. With the discovery of this illuminating document, revelations of the most unforeseen nature have been brought to light, confessions of the most intimate description have been exchanged, and what was once concealed is now revealed. And if some dirty laundry has been aired in the process, at least it is in the name of truth and justice, the twin virtues which served as guideposts in the lives of these two great men. Whatever transgressions they may inadvertently have committed have long been forgiven. There are family secrets here and to spare, enough to fill several additional drawers full of drawers. Both Conan Doyle and Sherlock Holmes have been stripped to their essentials, their souls laid bare, with more than one suppressed confidence discovered amongst the "unmentionables." I am inexpressibly grateful to have been afforded the opportunity to bring a long-lost manuscript to light and to be the conduit through whom a mystery has been solved and a friendship defined.

ALIBIS

by Bruce Harris

"And yet, Watson – and yet!"

The governess Grace Dunbar had a problem. All evidence pointed to her as Maria Gibson's killer. A fired gun, its bullet the same calibre as the one that killed Mrs. Gibson, was discovered in Dunbar's wardrobe. In addition, a note signed by Miss Dunbar was found with the dead woman. It confirmed an appointment between the two women, the location of which turned out to be the crime scene. Finally, Dunbar had a motive for killing Mrs. Gibson. The Gold King,

J. Neil Gibson was an attractive, wealthy man. He had shown an interest in Miss Dunbar. Robert W. Hahn astutely put it, "Even Hamilton Berger should have gotten a conviction on that evidence."1

Sherlock Holmes did not necessarily agree. He and Doctor Watson discussed the matter.

"Nor could she prove an alibi [italics added]. On the contrary, she had to admit that she was down near Thor Bridge – that was the scene of the tragedy – about that hour. She couldn't deny it, for some passing villager had seen her there."

"That really seems final," answers Watson.

"And yet, Watson – and yet!"

And yet, what? What exactly was Holmes thinking that put a doubt in his mind regarding Dunbar's guilt? Stealing a line from Inspector Bardle of the Sussex Constabulary (LION), "I wish I could see what was in your mind, Mr. Holmes." Before answering the question and fulfilling Bardle's wish, a cursory look at the word alibi in the Canon is prudent.

Alibi (in another place, elsewhere) was first used in 1731 2 The word appears only 11 times in the Canon (once each in THOR, SIGN, LION, RETI;

twice in SECO; and five times in WIST). Usually, the term alibi receives nothing more than a cursory mention. For example, in SIGN, Inspector Athelney Jones admits his mistake arresting Thaddeus Sholto for the murder of brother Bartholomew Sholto. Thaddeus had an unshakable alibi. "From the time he left his brother's room he was never out of sight of someone or other. So it could not be he who climbed over roofs and through trap-doors." It isn't clear if Thaddeus himself pleaded his case to Jones, or if Jones simply figured things out for himself.

Holmes provided Ian Murdoch's alibi in LION. Inspector Bardle ticked off the evidence against Murdoch for the murder of Fitzroy McPherson. First, the insubordinate Murdoch was known to have a short temper. Second, the two men had feuded. Lastly, both Murdoch and McPherson were suitors for the attention of the same woman, Maud Bellamy. Despite the evidence, Holmes convinced Bardle of Murdoch's innocence. "He had been with his scholars till the last moment, and within a few minutes of McPherson's appearance he came upon us from behind." The scholars, to which Holmes refers, were Murdoch's mathematics students at the prep school, The Gables.

Josiah Amberley's alibi falls apart in RETI. He claimed to have gone to the Haymarket Theatre without his wife (she had a headache according to Amberley). As proof, he provided his wife's unused theatre ticket from seat B-31. 3 But on the night in question, Holmes confirmed that the two seats on either side were unoccupied. The guilty Amberley was not where he said he was.

In SECO, valet John Mitton was cleared of Eduardo Lucas' murder because his alibi was "complete." In reality, Minton's alibi was weak. "He had visited friends in Hammersmith that night...It is true that he started home at an hour which should have brought him to Westminster before the time when the crime was discovered, but his own explanation that he had walked part of the way seemed probable enough in view of the fineness of the night." Does that describe a "complete" alibi? Hardly. In addition, some things belonging to the murdered Lucas were found among Mitton's things. Minton explained that, saying the items "...had been presents from the deceased." His statement was confirmed by the housekeeper, Mrs. Pringle. Interestingly, Mrs. Pringle's word goes unchallenged. It was taken as gospel.

In contrast, Aloysius Garcia apparently goes to extremes to befriend Scott Eccles in order to establish an alibi in WIST. This, despite the fact that his queer Surrey household consisted of an English-speaking servant and a cook. Either one, ala Mrs. Pringle in SECO, could have vouched for Garcia. Instead, Garcia invited Eccles, a newly acquired friend, to spend the night at his home. At 1:00am, Garcia asked Eccles if he had rung. According to Holmes, "...it was he [Garcia] who had arranged for the presence of Scott Eccles, which could only have been done for the purpose of an alibi."

Edward F. Clark, Jr, 4 and D. Martin Dakin 5 question the belief that Garcia's early morning visit to Eccles' bedroom was for the purpose of establishing a time-specific alibi. Garcia and company were driven by revenge. Whether it was justified, or his was a "criminal enterprise," is debatable. Holmes explained to Watson, "...only a man with a criminal enterprise desires to establish an alibi." The quote is a curious one, but it helps explain Holmes' thought process regarding Grace Dunbar's guilt or innocence.

As previously stated, the evidence against Grace Dunbar for murdering Maria Gibson in THOR was overwhelming. "And yet, Watson – and yet!" Holmes left the sentence unfinished. We can assume an unspoken name came into Holmes' mind that explained his train of thought: Albert de Commarin. In STUD, Holmes told Watson, "Lecoq was a miserable bungler." However, he said nothing of Lecoq's mentor, Pere Tabaretin Emile Gaboriau's, "The Lerouge Case." 6

In Gaboriau's story, Albert de Commarin, like Grace Dunbar, is the prime suspect in a murder case. The victim, the Widow Lerouge, was stabbed and killed by the sharpened end of a small sword. A broken tip distinguished the sword. de Commarin owned a similar broken foil. Other evidence, including a footprint uncovered at the crime scene matched de Commarin's boot. The remnants of a smoked cigar was found near the victim. It was the same brand smoked by de Commarin and the murderer had used a cigar holder similar to one used by de Commarin. His umbrella, trousers, and gloves all pointed toward de Commarin's guilt. Despite the irrefutable evidence, de Commarin offered no explanation. The absence of an alibi struck Tabaret as significant. He said to magistrate Daburon, "Not an alibi, nothing? No explanations? The idea! It is inconceivable! Not an alibi? We must then be mistaken. He cannot be the criminal. That is certain!" 7

Most chronologists agree THOR occurred in either 1900 or 1901. In Miss Dunbar's case, Holmes recalled Tabaret's words, uttered approximately 35 years earlier. This should not be surprising. In REDH, Holmes told Jabez Wilson and Watson, "...I am able to guide myself by the thousands of other similar cases which occur to my memory." Lacking an alibi, Grace Dunbar has Albert de Commarin and the sharp memory of the world's first consulting detective to thank for clearing her name of murder.

Notes

1 Robert W. Hahn, "Recount, Please, Mr. Holmes," Baker Street Journal, 26, No. 4, December 1976, 209-212, 210.

2 "Alibi." Merriam-Webster.com Dictionary, Merriam-Webster, https://www.merriam-webster.com/dictionary/alibi#h1.

3, William S. Baring-Gould provides a diagram from The Combined Atlas and Guide of London (1900), showing that seat 31 in B row of the upper circle at the Haymarket Theatre did not exist. See William S. Baring-Gould, The Annotated Sherlock Holmes, Volume II. Clarkson N. Potter, Inc: New York, 1967, 555.

4 Edward F. Clark, Jr., "'Wisteria Lodge' Revisited (A Model Cop, a Model Laundry Item, and a Not-So-Model Culinary Artist," Baker Street Journal, 31, No. 1, March, 1981, 24-31.

5 D. Martin Dakin, A Sherlock Holmes Commentary. Drake Publishers: New York, 1972.

6 For an enlightening comparison between Tabaret and Holmes, see LG Boulin, "The Missing Link, old Tabaret, and Ancestor of Sherlock Holmes," March 12, 2016, https://llunum.wixsite.com/lg-boulin/single-post/2016/03/12/The-missing-link-old-Tabaret-an-ancestor-of-SherlockHolmes. 7 Published serially in 1865 - 1866.

SHERLOCK HOLMES AND THE FRENCH CONNECTION

By Wendy Heyman-Marsaw

"To some extent," he answered thoughtfully, "my ancestors were country squires, who appear to have led much the same life as is natural to their class. But, none the less, my turn that way is in my veins, and may have come with my grandmother, who was the sister of Vernet, the French artist. Art in the blood is liable to take the strangest forms." "But how do you know it is hereditary?" "Because my brother Mycroft possesses it in a larger degree than I do."

- Sherlock Holmes in "The Greek Interpreter."

I have always been intrigued by Mr. Holmes' French ancestry. So little is known about him, that I took it upon myself to "investigate" the history of the Vernet family. I was almost overwhelmed with what I was able to discover. Here I share with you, dear reader, the essence of my labours.

(- Mrs. Hudson)

His sister was Camille Françoise Josephine Le Comte (nee' Vernet 1788-1858)

*Note from Wendy: Consider and compare these Canonical descriptions of Sherlock Holmes as you study Horace Vernet's image shown above: He had thin, firm, lips; steady grey eyes, particularly sharp and piercing, with a faraway introspective look when he was exerting his full powers; thin eager face; dolichocephalic skull (long narrow head); long thin nose, thin hawk-like nose; brows with well-marked supra-orbital development (brow ridge). Also note Horace Vernet's self-portrait.

Early Origins of the Vernet Family

The surname Vernet was first found in Ile-de-France, where the family had been prominent for centuries and held a family seat with lands and manor. Mr. Holmes used the term "country squires" to describe his ancestors. Squire is a British term for a country landowner or gentleman. Several members of the Vernet family distinguished themselves through their contributions towards the community in which they lived and were rewarded with lands and titles.

The Vernets - A Family of French Artists

Antoine Vernet (1689-1753) was a very successful artisan and decorative painter. His sons Jean-Antoine (1716-1755) painted seascapes and Antoine-François (1730-1779) was also a decorative painter. Another son, Claude Joseph (1714-1789), studied in Rome where he acquired an excellent reputation throughout Europe as a leading landscape and seascape artist. He was summoned to Paris in 1753 and was commissioned by King Louis XV to paint a famous series of seaports of France. His 14 completed works now hang in the Louvre.

Claude Joseph's son, Carle (b. Antoine Charles Horace 1758-1835) rose to fame during the empire with drawings of Napoleon Bonaparte's Italian campaign. The Battle of Marengo (which now hangs in Versailles) and Morning in Austerlitz are two of his best known works. Under the Restoration, he was also popular as a lithographer and painter of dogs, horses and scenes of the hunt. Carle never quite achieved the success of his father or his son, Horace (b. Emile Jean Horace 1789-1863). Carle was also father to Camille Françoise Josephine (1788-1858).

Camille and her brother Horace were born in the Louvre, where the family lived for a short time during the French Revolution in 1789 and 4 years hence. Little is known about Camille since she was overshadowed by her famous father, brother and husband, Hippolite Le Comte (1781-1857) – also an artist. Camille married Le Comte at the age of 19 in Paris. The couple had four children. Horace Vernet (b. Emile Jean Horace) who was a Bonapartist, quickly developed a disdain for the high-minded seriousness of academic French art, which was distinguished by subjects taken mostly from contemporary life. Instead he depicted masterful battle scenes and French soldiers in a familiar manner rather than the idealized fashion popular at the time. One painting that demonstrates his direct style is the "Dog of the Regiment Wounded".

He gained recognition during the early part of the Bourbon Restoration (1814-1830) and was granted many commissions by the future King Louis-Philippe. Critics marvelled at the incredible speed with which he painted. His paintings were also noted for their historical accuracy as well as their vivid landscapes. One anecdote maintains that when Horace was asked to remove a certain obnoxious general, he replied, "I am a painter of history, sire, and I will not violate the truth." (This comment reminds me of those made by Mr. Holmes during the course of his many adventures, since he is always dedicated to finding the truth in any problematic situation.) An example of Horace's style is the "The Battle of Hanau" (1824).

During the Restoration his studio was a centre of political intrigue as well as a meeting place for sportsmen and writers.

By 1826 he accomplished a great deal having been awarded a Cross of the Legion of Honour conferred by Napoleon Bonaparte, joining the Freemasons in England, and was elected to the Academie des Beaux-Artes. From 1825-1835 he was the Director of the French Academy of Rome. In 1835 he became a professor at the Academie des Beaux-Artes, a position he held for his lifetime.

The King requested Horace to paint a gallery of the fruits of colonization for Versailles. He travelled to Northern Africa in 1833.

1837 was the inauguration of the Historical Museum at Versailles. Three large scale Horace Vernet paintings were installed in the Gallery of Battles. He created a portrait of King Louis-Philippe with his sons posing in front of the gates of the palace.

Just 10 months after the invention of the daguerreotype, an intrigued Horace Vernet travelled to Egypt and Malta to take daguerreotypes which were converted into engravings for a book.

That same year he also travelled to Russia and spent almost 12 months with Tsar Nicholas I. He was also made a Commander of the Legion of Honour that year and by 1862 he was made a Grand Officer of the Legion of Honour.

And so ends my "investigation" of Mr. Sherlock and Mr. Mycroft Holmes' French ancestors, their grandmother, Camille Le Comte (nee' Vernet) and grand uncle, the artist Horace Vernet. I do hope it provides some answers to the questions surrounding their familial lineage. Art in the blood does, it appears, to be hereditary.

Horace Vernet is remembered by a street, Rue Horace Vernet, in the small town of Thouars in the Deux Sevres, France to this very day.

Recipes

Chicken Marengo - In mid-June 1800, Napoleon Bonaparte's troops were engaged in battle with Austrian forces near the small village of Marengo in northern Italy. The battle was fierce and Napoleon was both victorious and hungry. He asked his chef to prepare a meal quickly and the cook scoured the countryside looking for ingredients. He discovered a chicken, mushrooms, olive oil, tomatoes, herbs, eggs and crawfish. Within minutes, a fire was started, and the chef prepared a quick sauté of the chicken with tomatoes, mushrooms, oil and herbs. It is said that he garnished the dish before serving it with a fried egg and crawfish.

Serves 4 with rice and a tossed green salad.

Ingredients: 1 3-pound chicken cut into serving pieces, Salt to taste (if desired), freshly ground pepper, to taste, 2 Tbsp. butter, 2 Tbsp. olive oil, 1 ½ cups thinly sliced mushrooms (about 1/2 pound), ½ cup finely chopped onion, ½ tsp. finely minced garlic, 1 bay leaf, 2 sprigs fresh thyme or 1/2 tsp. dried, ½ cup dry white wine, 2 cups cored and cubed red ripe tomatoes (or use canned tomatoes), ¼ cup tomato paste, ½ cup chicken broth, 2 sprigs fresh parsley. Garnish with a fried egg and cooked crawfish (or substitute shrimp) as desired.

Mode: Sprinkle the chicken with salt and pepper to taste. Heat the butter and oil in a heavy skillet over medium-high heat. Add the chicken pieces skin-side down. Cook until golden brown on one side, about five minutes. Turn the pieces and cook on the other side about two minutes. Pour off the fat from the skillet. Scatter the mushrooms over the chicken. Stir to distribute. Add the onion, garlic, bay leaf and thyme and cook about 5 minutes. Add the wine and scrape the bottom of the skillet with a wooden spoon to dissolve the brown particles that cling to the bottom of the pan. Add the tomatoes, tomato paste, chicken broth and parsley. Bring to the boil. Cover and cook 10 minutes. Meanwhile cook the fried egg and crawfish or shrimp for a garnish if desired.

Beef Wellington –The Battle of Waterloo was fought on Sunday, 18 June 1815, near Waterloo in Belgium. Napoleon Bonaparte was defeated by a British-led coalition under the command of the Duke of Wellington. The battle marked the end of the Napoleonic Wars. This dish is actually French, but was re-named during the 19th Century wars with France. Serves 4. (Note: Beef Wellington was originally made with pate' de fois gras but has been modified since this ingredient is becoming increasingly rare. It is actually outlawed in some countries.) The recipe itself is adapted from Chef Gordon Ramsay.

Ingredients: 1 pound beef tenderloin filet, coarse & table salt and pepper, extra virgin olive oil, 1 pound mushrooms (half cremini, half shiitake is a nice combination), 4 thin slices ham (Parma or prosciutto), 2 Tbsp. yellow mustard (Coleman's Original English Mustard is good, as is a fine Dijon), 7 ounces puff pastry (needs 3 hours to defrost in refrigerator if using frozen), 2 egg yolks, beaten.

Mode: Season the fillet generously with table salt and pepper. Heat a tablespoon or two of oil in a large pan on high heat. Sear the fillet in a sauté pan on all sides until well browned (hint: do not move the fillet until it has had a chance to brown). Remove the filet from the pan and let cool. Once cooled, brush the fillet on all sides with mustard. Chop the mushrooms coarsely and put them into a food processor and purée. Heat the sauté pan on medium high heat. Transfer the mushroom purée into the pan and cook, allowing the mushrooms to release their moisture.

When the moisture released by the mushrooms has boiled away, remove the mushrooms from the pan and set aside to cool. Roll out a large piece of plastic wrap. Lay out the slices of ham on the plastic wrap so that they overlap. Spread the mushroom mixture over the ham. Place the beef filet in the middle, roll the mushroom and ham over the fillet, using the plastic wrap so that you do this tightly. Wrap up the beef filet into a tight barrel shape, twisting the ends of the plastic wrap to secure it. Refrigerate for 20 minutes. Preheat oven to 400°F. On a lightly floured surface, roll out the puff pastry sheet to a size that will wrap around the beef fillet. Unwrap the fillet from the plastic wrap and place in the middle of the pastry dough. Brush the edges of the pastry with the beaten egg yolks. Fold the pastry around the fillet, cutting off any excess at the ends (pastry that is more than 2 layers thick will not cook all the way, try to limit the overlap).

Place on a small plate, seam side down, and brush beaten egg yolks all over the top. Chill for 5-10 minutes. Place the pastry-wrapped fillet on a baking pan. Brush the exposed surface again with beaten eggs. Score the top of the pastry with a sharp knife, not going all the way through the pastry. Sprinkle the top with coarse salt. Bake at 400°F for 25-35 minutes. The pastry should be nicely golden when done. To ensure that your roast is medium rare, test with an instant read meat thermometer. Pull out at 125-130°F for medium rare. Remove from oven and let rest for 10 minutes before slicing. Slice in 1-inch thick slices.

(Mrs. Hudson Recommends: Available from www.mxpublishing.com & https://www.redbubble.com/shop/ap/51250666

With the 16th review from Publishers Weekly, the MX Book of New Sherlock Holmes Stories breaks more records. Over a dozen starred reviews for a single series is unprecedented.

"NOW LOOK HERE, CAPTAIN CROKER"

by Roger Johnson

A while back I came across Cruise of the 'Alert': Four Years in Patagonian, Polynesian, and Mascarene Waters (1878-82) by R.W. Coppinger, M.D. (Staff-Surgeon, Royal Navy, C.M.Z.S.), published by Swan Sonnenschein & Co. of London in 1883.

In Polynesia, the Alert called at Tonga, then usually referred to by the British as the Friendly Islands – a fact which made me wonder about Arthur Conan Doyle's choice of name for Jonathan Small's savage Andamanese companion. Was the name ironic, because Tonga, "the unhallowed dwarf with his hideous face, and his strong yellow teeth gnashing at us in the light of our lantern," was far from friendly in the eyes of Holmes and Watson? Or was it a sort of tribute to the little man's blazing loyalty? "He was stanch and true, was little Tonga. No man ever had a more faithful mate," said Small.

Then another significant and unusual name caught my attention. In Chapter VIII I read:

Tongatabu, Friendly Islands, 8th to 18th of November — The credit of discovering the Tonga Islands rests with Tasman, who saw them on the 20th of January, 1643, and subsequently anchored his ship on the north-west side of the large island. Tongatabu. Cook saw the islands during his second voyage in October 1773, and on his third voyage in 1777 he made a stay of three months at the group, for more than a month of which time he was anchored at Tongatabu, the principal and most southward island of the group. The islands were subsequently visited by D'Entrecasteaux, Maurelle (1781), Lieutenant Bligh of the Bounty. Captain Edwards of the Pandora (1791), and other explorers of the eighteenth century.

In the month of November 1806, an English privateer, the Port-au-Prince, arrived at Lifonga, one of the Hapai Islands, where the ship was seized by the natives, and most of the crew massacred. Among the few whose lives were spared was a young man named Mariner, who acquired the friendship of the chief, Finow, and lived peacefully with the natives for the space of four years, accumulating during that time a vast amount of information concerning their manners and habits. Mariner's narrative was subsequently published in a book written by Dr. John Martin, which is still regarded as the standard work on the Tonga Islands.

The Wesleyan missionaries established themselves here in the year 1822 and were well received: and some years subsequently a French Roman Catholic mission was also successfully established. At the time of our visit the entire population of the Tonga Islands, including Tongatabu, Hapai, and Vavau, amounted to 25,000, while that of Tongatabu alone was 12,000. Of the latter number, 8.000 belonged to the Wesleyan, and 4.000 to the Catholic, Church.

We anchored in the harbour of Tongatabu, off the town of Nukualofa, on the 8th of November, at about midday. The anchorage looked very bare indeed, there being only one vessel beside ours, a merchant barque belonging to Godeffroy and Co., of Hamburg, the well-known South Sea Island traders.

The most striking objects on shore, as viewed from our position in the anchorage, were the Wesleyan Church — an old dilapidated wooden building crowning the summit of a round-topped hill, about sixty feet high, and said to be the highest point on the island — and the king's palace, a very neat-looking villa-edifice abounding in plate-glass windows, and surrounded by a low wall, in which remained two breaches, intended for the reception of massive iron gates, which, through a series of untoward circumstances, are not likely to be ever placed in position. It appears that some time ago the king gave a carte blanche order for two pairs of gates to be sent out from England. and when, after a long series of delays, owing to mistakes in the shipping arrangements, they at length reached Tongatabu, he was rather unpleasantly surprised to find that the excessive charges for freightage had run up the entire cost to the sum of £800. They were then found to be so large and massive as to be quite unsuited for the purpose for which they were intended, so they were thrown down on the ground in a disjointed condition, where they now lie, rusting and half-buried in weeds. Somewhat in the rear of the royal palace is seen a rather imposing private dwelling-house, the residence of Mr. Baker, formerly a Wesleyan minister, and now the political prime minister of the kingdom.

In the afternoon some of us walked out to see the old, fortified town of Bea, which is distant from Nukualofa about four miles in a southerly direction, and is reached by a very good cart-road. This town — or, more properly speaking, village, for it is now but thinly populated — was formerly the stronghold of a party of Tongans, who objected to the introduction of Christianity, and were consequently obliged to defend themselves against the followers of the Wesleyan missionaries. The village is encircled by a rampart and moat, which have for many years past been allowed to go to decay, so that the moat is now partly obliterated with weeds and rubbish, and the strong palisades, which in former times added considerably to the defensive strength of the ramparts, have almost entirely disappeared.

As we entered the village by a cutting which pierced the ramparts on the north side, we saw the spot where Captain Croker, of H.M.S. Favourite, was shot down in 1848, when heading an armed party of bluejackets, with whom he was assisting the missionary party in an attack upon the irreconcilables. It seems to have been altogether a most disastrous and ill-advised undertaking. and of its effects some traces still remain in an assumption of physical superiority over their white fellow-creatures, which may be seen among some of the Tongans.

Not just Croker, please note, but Captain Croker. American texts give Lady Brackenstall's stalwart lover an extra letter, making him "Captain Crocker", but British readers have always known him as Captain Croker. Given Mary Brackenstall's antipodean origins, it seems at least possible that Arthur Conan Doyle deliberately named her *preux chevalier* after a sea captain with connections to the southern hemisphere.

The possibility edges towards probability when we realise that Captain Walter Croker of the Favourite sailed for Tonga from Sydney, New South Wales.

Here is the report of his death, with spelling as in the original, from the Australasian Chronicle for the 28th July 1840, published in Sydney: *

DEATH OF CAPTAIN CROKER OF H.M.S. FAVORITE.

In our last number we gave a brief notice of this melancholy event; we will now proceed to lay before our readers a more detailed account of the affray by which it was occasioned.

Upon the arrival of the Favorite at the Island of Tonga, or es it is more commonly called Tongataboo (Tonga the sacred), its inhabitants were engaged in an internal war, being divided into two opposite parties; namely, the Christians, or followers of the Methodist missionaries, and the heathen, of those retaining the ancient religion of the island, who were under the control and guidance of a Welshman, generally known by the cognomen of "Jemmy the Devil." 'The latter party had entrenched themselves in a strong fortress or stockade, to the great annoyance it appears of the Wesleyans and their disciples. These applied to the Favorite for assistance, which was almost immediately granted, and a considerable number of the crew immediately offered themselves as volunteers fur the expedition.

To facilitate the destruction of the fort three guns were brought ashore from the vessel, and planted on an eminence immediately fronting its walls, where the British also posted themselves, attended by a large party of the Christian natives. Soon after this a parley was agreed upon between the belligerent parties, in consequence of which the heathen leader (Jemmy the Devil) came out and held a consultation with Captain Croker, who upon seeing him approach him cried out "Well, Jemmy, I am happy to find you are willing to come to terms ; what can I do for you ?" to which the other replied "You can do a great deal if you like ;" alluding probably to the punishment which he would receive if he fell into the hands of that gentleman. The Captain then informed him that the only terms upon which peace could be restored would be to level with the ground the fortifications which had been raised by both parties, and to return to their former state of friendly intercourse, upon which the heathen champion requested half an hour to consult the native chiefs and return an answer, which was granted. The worthy envoy accordingly retired to his companions, but before the time had expired a message was sent from the fort, expressly stating that the heathen party were not willing to held intercourse with their enemies the Christian natives.

At the expiration therefore of the appointed period a fire was opened on the fort by the guns brought from the Favorite, after which the Christian party headed by Captain Croker, advanced to within 150 yards of the gate, where the fire of the besieged became so galling that the native Christians thought it advisable to decamp, for the purpose as they said of attacking the fort on the other side, but really with the intention of saving their carcasses from the destructive fire of the enemy, who, ensconced as they were behind the strong walls of the stockades, were enabled to pour a murderous fire through the loopholes upon the besieging party without receiving a shot in return.

The British then advanced under the order of their commander to the very walls of the fort, with the view of endeavouring to carry it by storm, but the fire of the besieged was so galling, that notwithstanding the gallantry with which the attack was commenced it was found impossible to proceed.

The death of Captain Croker—who received a rifle ball in the left breast, which passed through his heart while leaning against a tree, and suffering from extreme weakness occasioned by loss of blood from previous wounds—operated as the signal for abandoning the attempt, and the British accordingly fled to the ship, bearing with them those who had been killed or wounded in the action, but abandoning their guns and ammunition, which were almost immediately taken possession of by the enemy. The contest lasted about twenty minutes, and the loss of the British was the captain, the chief gunner's mate, and a quarter master killed, together with the first lieutenant (Mr. Dunlop) and nineteen others wounded. The two Wesleyan missionaries who had been previously residing on the island immediately went on board the Favorite which left them at Vavou, and afterwards proceeded onwards to Sydney. The above is all that appears to be yet known of this affair. The general impression is that the attack was as unadvised, as it was certainly ill-conducted, and much blame is attributed to the conduct of the missionaries for having kept alive the hostility which led to it.

At least there was the prospect of shared happiness for Captain Jack Croker of the Adelaide-Southampton Line and the former Mary Fraser.

Accessible online at

https://trove.nla.gov.au/newspaper/article/3172881

A NOTE ON NICOTINE

By Kelvin I. Jones

"I believe. . . he is a first-class chemist. . ." Stamford, STUD

At the time of Watson's first meeting with Holmes, the latter was studying at St. Bart's Hospital on a free-lance basis ("he has never taken out any systematic medical classes" – STUD) and had just discovered "the most practical medico-legal discovery for years ... an infallible test for bloodstains." Holmes admits to Watson that he dabbles "with poisons a great deal" and Stamford earlier comments, "I could imagine his giving a friend a little pinch of the latest vegetable alkaloid . . . simply ... to have an accurate idea of its effects." (STUD).

This youthful preoccupation with vegetable alkaloids was, I believe, not merely objective. There were both personal and scientific reasons why Holmes took a keen interest in alkaloids. The compounds obtained from vegetable alkaloids (morphine, nicotine, quinine, caffeine, etc.) produce some of the strongest poisons known to man. Holmes, with his wayward knowledge, had clearly spent time at Bart's investigating a fascinating branch of learning where the gaps were still to be filled by subsequent pharmacologists.

Holmes admitted to his faithful chronicler that drugs were a way of assisting his mental faculties. "My mind is like a racing engine," he claimed, "tearing itself to pieces..." Cocaine, nicotine and morphine provided for the great neurasthenic detective the perfect answer. Cocaine is an "upper," morphine a "downer," and nicotine is also a depressant. With these drugs at his disposal, he could regulate his own metabolism, pushing it beyond its normal bounds. Instances of extraordinary activity contrast sharply with those of great languor. Compare these passages, for example:

"See the foxhound with hanging ears and drooping tail . . . and compare it with the same hound as, with gleaming eyes and straining muscles, it runs upon a breast high scent – such was the change in Holmes since the morning."

"Holmes had spent several days in bed, as was his habit from time to time. . ." And, in SIGN, Watson reminds us:

"He was bright, eager, and in excellent spirits, a mood which in his case alternated with fits of the blackest depression."

What Holmes was aiming for was that "equanimity of feeling" first described as a reaction to the drug opium. As De Quincey observed:

"Whereas wine disorders the mental faculties, opium . . . introduces amongst them the most exquisite order, legislation and harmony, ... it communicates serenity and equipoise to all the faculties ..."

De Quincey abjured the use of alcohol. We note also that Holmes was supposedly no great user of the drug (TWIS – although I do believe he may not have been telling Watson the whole truth. See my notes in 'The Ultimate Sherlock Holmes Smoking Companion'. *On the other hand, he overindulged his taste for nicotine. The reason is fairly obvious, although it has only recently been pointed out.

In the brain, nervous impulses are transmitted from one cell to another because of the release at nerve endings of what is known as neuro-transmitters. Nicotine imitates this action. Tests on animals have confirmed the opinion of heavy smokers that smoking may prevent drowsiness and facilitate mental concentration. Holmes undoubtedly wanted rapid results from his alkaloids. The cocaine would certainly have given him that, for its effect is instantaneous. Morphine, on the other hand, has a much slower reaction. Holmes, in his study of alkaloids, made use of himself in these experiments as a guinea pig, but clearly developed an addiction for the "hard" drugs.

But the question remains – exactly how did he get onto the drugs in the first place? The answer, I believe, lies in the early period of his life about which we know so little.

In his youth or late adolescence, Sherlock Holmes may have suffered from a particularly painful malady that required the use of morphine (this was probably administered in its more popular form, laudanum). I base this assertion on clear indications in the Canon.

Holmes, it appears, was his own worst enemy. His "iron constitution" was frequently pushed to the limits by his own reckless attitude to work. In REIG we learn that he had been working for a period "extending over two months ... he had never worked less than fifteen hours a day." It has also been suggested that Holmes may have been slightly consumptive as a youth. The lean figure, coupled with a pale ascetic countenance, would seem to confirm this view.

But in conclusion, I do not think it was consumption which led him to the morphine bottle, and those long hours spent at St. Bart's, investigating the properties of obscure alkaloids. It was probably something quite serious, a disorder of the abdominal organs which incommoded him for much of his life. Morphine was vital in keeping Holmes's grip on his professional career whilst suffering this encumbrance. The drug is, of course, a spinal stimulant, obliterating pain more effectively than any other known rival and supplying a dreamless sleep.

Much of Holmes's behaviour can be explained by recourse to this theory of an abdominal disability: the inability to sleep or keep regular hours, the irregular eating habits, the irritability and intolerance of others. All these symptoms point to some longstanding disease which dogged the detective throughout his years in practice.

The morphine supplied a dual-edged solution, for in his middle years, Holmes discovered that he had become a hopeless addict, suffering the accompanying displeasures of constipation, loss of energy, heavy dependence, etc. It was left to his best and wisest friend. Dr John H. Watson, to supply an antidote and "wean" him from that terrible route downwards to the realms of Morpheus.

The last link in the chain is provided for us in EMPT where, in Holmes's own words, he "spent some months in a research into coal tar derivatives." This research was carried out in the French town of Montpelier in 1894.

What was it that Holmes was after? One commentator has suggested that he was probing for the discovery of plastics, but chronologically this would not have been possible. The coal-tar derivatives consist of a number of aromatic carbon compounds. They are: benzene (used in the manufacture of plastics), naphthalene, anthracene, phenol (an antiseptic), toluene, aniline and pyridine. It is the last of these derivatives which, I believe, gives us an insight into Holmes's motivation for his research. For pyridine is an odourless liquid base got from the dry distillation of coal-tar. There is also a derivative of pyridine and that is nicotinic acid. Now this chemical is a white crystalline substance formed by the oxidation of nicotine. Moreover, it is a vitamin of the "B" group and has been found vital to the treatment of pellagra, a deficiency disease characterized by cracking of the skin. In unchecked cases, the disease can often end in insanity.

Did Holmes suffer from this disease and was he looking for a cure? I believe so, for one of the unfortunate results of long-term drug addiction, is a corresponding loss of vitamin balance in the body. When the dietary requirements of the body are disturbed over a long period, a disease like pellagra is more than possible.

NOTES

*'The Sign of Four,' is much preoccupied with drugs and drug taking. Indeed, the first chapter of Watson's narrative is almost entirely devoted to Homes' explanation of why he uses cocaine and morphine. Readers at the time who read their editions of 'Lippincott's Magazine' would have regarded both Oscar Wilde's Dorian Gray and Sherlock Holmes as 'Bohemians', a

widely used concept which had connotations of decadence, self – indulgence, 'art for art's sake' and 'fin de siècle.' Wilde himself believed that he was witnessing the end of civilization, and that it was a period of decadence, much like the latter days of the Roman Empire. Apart from drugs and art, what else was there to enjoy during those declining days of an Empire which had grown glutinous and terminally exploitative?

The public must have shuddered at these descriptions and imagined areas such as London's docklands, and the East End, to be opium-drenched, exotic and dangerous places.

The den visited by Holmes and Watson was situated in Upper Swandam Lane, in Rotherhithe. As a youth, I often cycled from my home in Lewisham to Rotherhithe, which was still then a place of gaunt red brick warehouses, interspersed with small public houses and residential buildings. Here I discovered several likely contenders for the opium den of TWIS, with a basement and upper floor at the back of which doors opened to convey goods onto barges.

What puzzled me at the time when I first read Dr Watson's account, and what still intrigues me now, is Holmes' comment to his chronicler about his familiarity with the opium den: 'Had I been recognised in that den my life would not have been worth an hour's purchase; for I have used it before now for my own purposes, and the rascally Lascar who runs it has sworn to have vengeance upon me. There is a trap door at the back of that building, near the corner of Paul's Wharf, which could tell some strange tales of what has passed through it upon the moonless nights.'

Exactly what does Holmes mean by telling Watson that he has used the place 'before now for my own purposes'? Does it mean that he has used the den for recreational opium smoking? Or is he referring to some undercover work which in the past has necessitated his visiting the den in a disguise? Both would imply that he stayed on the premises, smoking amounts of opium very much unspecified.

THE LINCOLN STREET MINISTER

by David Marcum

In spite of my careful attempts to dress accordingly, I couldn't help but sense that my clothes, as ragged as they were, were still too prosperous in appearance for this locality.

Sherlock Holmes and I stood back from the pavement, doing our best to appear as idle loungers while we observed the building across the street and a few doors to the north. While I had long ago taken to saving a number of my older garments for tasks such as this – those worn by age, out of style, or damaged during events of some of Holmes's investigations – I still felt that I looked too much like myself, while Holmes had managed – as always – to seemingly become another person entirely.

We were halfway down Lincoln Street, in Whitechapel, and the various efforts to improve the district following the Ripper murders of a decade earlier had not yet reached this thoroughfare. That short lane was uniquely located between the Whitechapel Union Workhouse to the west, the City of London Union Infirmary to the east, and a mortuary and the vast Tower Hamlets Cemetery to the south. The opening to Mile End Road at the north seemed to be the only way to escape what the rest of the surroundings implied – but there were, in fact, two other forms of figurative escape in Lincoln Street, both of a more inward-directed turn.

Near the north end of the street was a shabby public house, long a fixture here, where many locals congregated to numb their daily existence. And located just beside it was a new establishment in an old structure, the recently congregated Church of the Impoverished Souls, led by London's latest nine-day wonder, Reverend Philo Tate Simmons.

The man had first come to the public's notice several months before, when London was trapped in a hot and tedious summer. Mid-August had brought temperatures of nearly one-hundred degrees – tolerable to an old Afghan fighter like myself, but deadly at times to the average British citizen.

In the midst of that, a man had begun to minister to those in need – serving cool water to passers-by in Trafalgar Square. At first he had been just another of several performing similar functions, and he would have passed unnoticed had he not also begun to perform miracles.

The word spread about him, dressed in black in the deadly summer heat. I had tarried once to watch him as I went from one place to another on an irrelevant errand. He was a big fellow, his greying hair rather long and frequently pushed straight back from his high brow, only to slip down again as he bent to assist the next person, and the next and the next. The stories began to be discussed and shared more frequently, along with his name and apparent American origins, when the sick and lame would timidly approach, only to receive his prayers and touch and soft words, allowing them to rise and walk away, loudly proclaiming that they were healed of their afflictions.

I recall at the time taking the cynical view that the "healed" individuals were his cronies, hired to perform this little bit of dumb crambo for those who were gullible and susceptible to drama, and had money to lose, but one saw such every day, and it made no lasting impression. At some point around the turning toward cooler weather, I again became aware of Simmons, having read a short piece about him in one of the daily newspapers. Once more, I confess that I didn't pay too much attention, having encountered another one of his apparent faith-healing ilk long ago, during a boyhood journey to the United States. I did note that Simmons had now parlayed his new fame into obtaining a physical building in Whitechapel to be used as a church, seemingly by way of an enthusiastic patron. I recall nothing else from the account, and quickly passed along to other stories of greater interest.

I had no notion whether Holmes was aware of Pastor Simmons until one morning in late October of '98, when we had a visitor from Mr. Thaddeus Hellifield, the noted banker and Royal advisor. This, I would soon learn, was the pastor's reluctant and indirect patron, involuntarily by way of his only child, a daughter.

"I fear that I've been fleeced, Mr. Holmes," he said, settling himself in the basket chair before the fire, his leg stiff and apparently resulting from old pain, as shown by the wince of his eyes and the strong but well-used old cane that he kept by his side. He squinted slightly at my friend, who had the window beside the chemical corner at his back. It was always Holmes's custom, when he was able, to arrange things in this way, so that he could closely examine his clients while his own face was somewhat obscured, particularly in the mornings when the eastern light was on that side of the building. It had been of use to him on many occasions, including the affair of the Newby Bridge scandal, which had started with a small but deceitful conversation and had spiralled into an affair that threatened a half-dozen noble houses, and also the matter of the woman from Margate, whose awareness of Holmes's little trick with the light, and her ability to place herself in a different seat, had in itself been a clue as to her intentions.

Hellifield had arrived at the time indicated in his note sent the night before, asking for an appointment but declining to provide a reason. His position and standing were enough to gain him entrance, but if his case hadn't interested Holmes, he would have soon been invited to leave. I'll admit that I expected to hear some tedious tale of boardroom shenanigans involving comparisons of ledgers and serendipitously fortuitous identifications of discrepancies – which was not the tale Hellifield told us at all.

"You'll know of this minister chap, Simmons," he said, having accepted the offer of hot coffee. "He's been getting a lot of attention lately. I first heard about him from my daughter, Lydia, back in the summer. In the last few months, she began to have an interest in that sort of thing – volunteering to help the poor, and so on. I've no quarrel with it, although Lydia seemed to think that I might when she first brought it up. We've always been at odds, you see. Rather surprised her that I didn't immediately forbid it. The truth is, after her mother died last year, I've really had no idea what to do with her, and when she found her way to this kind of thing, I was glad enough of it. Gave her something to do. I'll admit it taints her dinner conversation a bit when she starts floating those socialist ideas – she tends to get a bit shrill about it all – but thank heavens she doesn't seem to care a jot about being a suffragist.

"She could have worked with any number of organizations to help the sick, the poor, the lame, the lazy, and the downtrodden – far too many of them in London, as you're aware. The poor people, you know, not the organizations. No fault of their own, of course. At least not some of them. The poor veterans, for instance, and the ones who have no self-control – I pity them. I do. It's the ones who prey on them that I despise. I've heard tales of such things, and not just the sanitized versions of stories that Lydia brings home. After all, gentlemen, one would have to be a fool not to see the terrible underside of things. The Bank of England, for instance – settled in that little hub of ground that controls the richest parts of the Empire – is just a few thousand feet from Spitalfields and Whitechapel, for heaven's sake! The richest rubbing up against the worst of the worst. I was part of a group enlisted to take a look at these things five years or so ago. I know how things are. I'm not willingly blind like so many of my colleagues.

"That's why I've tried to help when I can – especially lately, based on Lydia's reports of where my resources can best be applied. I'm not foolish about it, though. I could give away my whole fortune to the poor tomorrow, and it would only be a bandage – and a poor one at that. There would be just as many of them needing help the next day. That's why I try to do what I do intelligently, and when Lydia said a good word for this American preacher, I was glad to help. It was little enough what he wanted – the funds to rent a broken-down building he's found for a small church. I provided them, for Lydia to pay the rent – on Lincoln Street, in Whitechapel."

I could see that Holmes was becoming impatient, and the fact was not lost on Hellifield, who hadn't obtained his position by being oblivious.

"Simmons has been there for just a month – since mid-September – and all reports are that he's settled in and is doing what one would expect: Giving sermons, serving up meals and medical comfort. Trying to provide opportunities for those who haven't had any and preach some sense to those who will listen. Something like the Salvation Army, I suppose – and it's no knock on Simmons to think that a better and established group like that might be more effective than he is, at least at present. There's plenty of work for all of them.

"But Lydia seems a bit too . . . involved with this one. At first I put it down to the enthusiasm of starting a new project and seeing it come to life. But it's more than that. I can see a gleam in her eyes when she talks about this American." He pursed his lips. His town lowered. He's reached his concern. "I think that she's in love with him."

Hellifield looked from one to the other of us, trying to elicit some sort of comment. I could imagine what Holmes might say – how this story appeared to be rooted in a father's disapproval of a man that his daughter might marry, and how this was nothing with which he could – or would – become involved. Hellifield's next comment seemed to confirm the direction of the consultation.

"The man is more than twice her age!" he erupted, his fists clenched and his face suddenly red at the thought. "He's quite likely around my age!"

Holmes uncrossed his legs and put his feet together on the floor, apparently preparing to stand. "Mr. Hellifield – " he began, but the banker raised a hand.

"I know what you're thinking. That I want you to find something about the man to convince my daughter he's not the one. I don't need you for that, Mr. Holmes. I have a dozen agents who are already working on that problem – quite discreetly. No, I came to you because I need a specialist. I need you to expose him as a fraud – so that Lydia will see him as he truly is."

Holmes shook his head, but he settled back into his chair. "I typically don't involve myself in debunking ministers – "

"But you do!" interrupted Hellifield. "I've asked around about you. You're right. You don't go after ministers per se – at least not that I know of – who are associated with churches, but you do stop those people who prey on the gullible. How many false mediums and spiritualists have you exposed? I've read about several in the newspapers, and I'm sure that for everyone reported there were three others that weren't. I recall that business on Great Wild Street last year, in which the Prime Minister's cousin was so nearly arrested after his affair with the ectoplasmic woman – it's common knowledge to some of us in certain circles, you see, in spite of the PM's attempts to keep it quiet – and then there was the story your own brother told me about those girls kept prisoner by that supposed clairvoyant in the Waldeck Buildings in Ethelm Street. What makes them any different from exposing this Simmons and his parlour tricks?"

"The men you referenced," said Holmes, "didn't also found a church and feed the hungry and provide medical care to those in need. I keep an eye on things like this, and I've heard no reports of any questionable aspects of Simmons' ministry."

"So far," countered Hellifield. "Maybe he's as sound as the pound. Or maybe it's all a tactical manoeuvre to attract and wed a rich man's daughter – and my Lydia was the one caught in his net. Or possibly he never intended it that way, but in her fascination, she pushed herself into his sphere, and now that she's under his influence, perhaps he's changed his objectives."

"Have you discussed it with her?" I asked. "And have you met Simmons in person, and talked with him as well?"

"I have not," said Hellifield emphatically. "Lydia is headstrong. She's always been rebellious – natural enough, I suppose, but why give her ideas if they aren't there already? If she isn't in fact interested in this man, why suggest it as a possibility? And until I have all my facts straight, I'm not going to meet with Simmons either."

He turned to Holmes. "What I need is for you to investigate his claims to having this . . . supernatural power – this ability to heal the lame – in the same way you would one of these mediums who take money from the overcredulous and then put on a show in the dark with floating trumpets and knocking tables." He sat forward on his seat. "Don't think about it as me asking you to vet my daughter's suitor. Instead, consider if he's some American con-man who is taking advantage of those who don't know better, and can't afford it."

Holmes pondered for a moment, and I was wagering with myself which way he would lean. It could, I decided, go either way. Holmes had a marked distaste for charlatans, and had often gone to extra effort for no substantive reward when he perceived that one of them needed to be exposed. But as he'd pointed out, in this case the man seemed to be doing some good work – at least it seemed that way on the surface. I found myself wishing that he didn't dismiss Hellifield, as I suddenly wanted to know more about this man Simmons, and in spite of years of seeing some of the worst from people, I also hoped in a small and secret way that somehow Simmons's abilities would be confirmed – or if not that, at least not entirely discredited.

Finally, Holmes nodded. "I'll look into the matter, with the understanding that I have no preconceived agenda."

Hellifield nodded and pulled himself to his feet. From what I'd observed when he walked in, and now as he braced himself upright with his old, battered cane, that he suffered from some sort of hip dysplasia of long standing. It was reflected by the uneven wear of his shoes.

"That's all I can ask," he said. "Now that you're on board, I'd like to direct you to one of Simmons' services tonight. I have a little something in mind that might force the issue one way or the other."

Holmes raised an eyebrow and started to object. "I would advise that you let me make some inquiries before you begin changing the conditions of the test – " he said before Hellifield interrupted.

"No, no. I won't affect what you're doing, but it will give us something to think about. The service usually starts about seven." And then, despite Holmes's further attempts to elicit an explanation, he departed.

When we'd heard the front door close, Holmes looked at me. "You're features are all-too-obvious. You hope that Father Christmas will prove to be real."

I smiled. "Well, who couldn't use a little more goodness in the world? And magic as well."

Holmes wagged a finger. "Be careful, Watson. Some of these religious types don't want their magic to be categorized in the same way as a witch doctor's magic, in spite of the obvious similarities. And in any case, it's yet to be determined just how much of a con-man this Simmons fellow is."

"Now you're theorizing in advance of the data," I countered. "You've declared him guilty before proven innocent."

He stood. "So I have, which shows that even after decades of personal discipline, it's far too easy to be tempted into a lapse of thinking." He walked to the door, pausing to retrieve his Inverness and fore-and-aft cap. "Are you available this evening to attend tonight's performance at Simmons' church?"

I averred that I was.

"Excellent. I'll see some people and ask some questions, and send word about the arrangements." And with that he departed.

I spent the afternoon writing, making a record of our recent foray into Fynes Street, the dramatic rescue of Dr. Copper's daughter from the political vivisectionist, and the running battle that followed north into Westminster, terminating on that low wall separating the Victoria Tower Gardens from the river. The abrasions on my knuckles had nearly healed, but the politician's secretary – a killer of unusual stealth – wouldn't soon recover from the fall he took off the wall and onto the jagged debris standing in the mud beneath, revealed by the river's low tide. Whether he walked or was wheeled to the gallows was still an open question.

It was nearly five when Holmes sent word as to where we should meet in Lincoln Street, while advising that I wear old clothes to somewhat fit in. I complied, arriving at around six-thirty, where I joined my friend is a little-noticed doorway where we could see the relatively new church of Philo Tate Simmons, late of the United States.

"My afternoon was an exercise in futility," Holmes informed me as we watched men and women in various conditions of financial distress file into Simmons' makeshift church. Seeing that his clothing was so much different than what he was wearing when he departed Baker Street, I concluded that he'd visited one of his various hidey holes to take on a disguise. "I only found shaky confirmation of his 'miracles', and no argument to provide weight to an argument on the other side."

"Are you approaching the task as if you haven't looked deeply enough unless you find something negative to report?"

"Not necessarily, but one would have expected to discover something questionable. Through various American resources, I obtained a basic biography of the fellow. Born in 1853 in Johnson's Depot, in north-eastern Tennessee. Worked for a number of years as a labourer for his father-in-law – yes, he was married once, apparently to a girl from the same small town where he was born. She died during childbirth in the early eighties – 1883 I believe – at which point Simmons underwent some sort of religious conversion, becoming an itinerant minister, slowly working his way north and east, until he ended up in New York City a couple of years ago."

"Your American sources were quite effective, considering the only had a few hours to assemble their report."

"I accept this information with a grain of wariness. Apparently after Simmons arrived in New York, he came to the attention of a newspaper reporter, attracted by the street-side healings that were being performed for the lowliest of the citizens. This reporter spent a few weeks last year researching Simmons' past, even going so far as to travel along the man's trail back to Tennessee, where he interviewed some of the early actors in the story. It should be noted that Simmons spent years moving from one place to another, sometimes serving as a minister at a church in a little town before abandoning it and taking to the road once more. The reporter found no indications of any questionable behaviour, and was unable to verify when the healings first began. Simmons wasn't doing anything like that in his home town – no turning the water to wine at his own wedding, for instance – so it started sometime during his travels at an unimportant stop along the way. In the middle of this year, he unexpectedly announced the call to carry his ministry to London, and here we are."

"You mentioned 'shaky confirmation' of his miracles. Did that come from the reporter's story?"

"No. The fellow mentioned a few that he'd personally witnessed, but there was no apparent effort to speak with anyone who had actually been healed. I questioned some of my acquaintances who loiter around Trafalgar Square, seeing if they were familiar with anyone who had received a 'treatment' from the minister. For instance, Pete Byers' patch is set up near the location where Simmons' handed out water, and he didn't recognize any of the people who approached and asked for the minister's touch, before walking away rejoicing."

I knew Pete Byers of old, as he was one of the first people that I'd met in mid-1881 while becoming associated with Holmes's unique consulting practice. Those who knew Byers weren't fooled by his game, but visitors to the city were mightily impressed with his spurious artistic efforts and tossed substantial coinage his way, circumventing the begging laws in the same way that a street busker earns donations by offering an actual effort – although Byers' effort was in the wasted labour he spent each day rather than in actual creation. Early each morning he wheeled a covered barrow to a fixed spot in Trafalgar Square. Then, keeping the barrow's contents shielded by a tarpaulin, he moved what he carried to a fixed spot on the street. After crawling under the tarp and hiding under it for a few minutes, as if he were doing something important, he would emerge and, waiting for a moment where there was a lull in foot traffic, gently remove the covering to reveal a life-sized sleeping dog, seemingly sculpted from sand, as one would build a castle at the seaside. But in fact the tan-coloured sculpture, meant to seem fragile and temporary, was cast as a solid and movable piece, easily transported to the Square in the morning and loaded up again at night for removal to Byers' lodgings.

I remember when Holmes had first introduced me to Byers. We had approached the fellow as he rested on his knees, leaning forward and gently smoothing the back of the sand dog with a cloth dampened from a nearby bucket of water, as if carefully shaping it toward some higher level of perfection. There were several buckets of sand standing nearby, apparently the raw materials of this ephemeral art. When Byers saw us he bounced up, and I wondered how he could kneel on the pavement for so long without destroying his knees. His eyes twinkled as I praised his mastery of the sand sculpture, and I tossed him a coin, for which I received a sincere and chipper "Thank you!" Holmes didn't see fit to tell me the truth of it until we were walking down the Strand toward Simpson's, where we intended to celebrate the recent conclusion of the Jermyn Street assault by spending some of Holmes's fee.

"He pretends to smooth it like that all day long," said Holmes. "Those who regularly pass by, including the constables, know the sculpture for what it is – it never changes – but for someone new to the city, watching for just a few minutes before impatiently walking on, or only visiting for the day, it seems to be a remarkable bit of artistry, and Byers regularly makes a daily wage through his futile pantomime of sculpting to feed a jolly wife and six fat happy children."

As we stood before Simmons' church that night in '98, it had been nearly two decades since I'd met Byers, and he still worked that same bit of pavement, six days per week. I suspected that he'd had to replace his sand-cast dog in the meantime, but I'd never bothered to find out for sure. I suppose there are worse jobs, but I had convinced Byers early on to set out some padding for his knees, although nothing could be done about the gradual curve of his spine that permanently formed from leaning over so often and continuing to lightly conduct his faux labours on the tan sculpted dog.

'It's a wonder," I said, "that Byers didn't rise up and ask for Simmons to heal him. I know for a fact that he's in constant pain."

"It never crossed his mind," said Holmes. "I asked him about that this afternoon. He did wander over to have some water, but a man in his profession simply doesn't give any credence to the possibility that Simmons' actions could be honest. But as I said, he did confirm that none of the 'healed' were people that he knew – those who would be likely to be hired to pretend to be healed and drum up interest in whatever Simmons might have intended. They seemed genuinely ill, and then genuinely better, and genuinely grateful as well."

I tapped Holmes on the arm, having observed a distinctly different visitor entering the church across the street. "I see him," Holmes replied.

It was our client, Thaddeus Hellifield, painfully approaching the steps leading up to the church's front door, slowly working his way forward with the use of his stout cane. Like me, he was wearing old clothes in an attempt to fit into the surrounding neighbourhood, but he had done even worse than me in succeeding. The shine on his shoes was visible even where we stood, and his hair was too carefully barbered to fit in with those who passed him toward the entrance.

Glancing to make sure the street was clear, Holmes set out toward the church, and I followed. Hellifield perceived our approach and he turned toward Holmes, whom he did not immediately recognize. My disguise, however, was less successful, and the man smiled. "I'm glad you're here," he said.

"You mentioned," countered Holmes softly, "that you have 'something in mind that might force the issue one way or the other'."

"I do. I could have hired someone else to do it, but why pay a man to do what you can do better yourself?" He gestured toward the doorway. "It's nearly time for the service to begin. Shall we?"

We climbed the steps, and I could tell that Hellifield wouldn't appreciate any assistance. As we matched his slow pace, I was able to study the old building. It wasn't a house as I'd first perceived, but rather one of the old buildings constructed for use by the different guilds that had been scattered throughout Whitechapel in long-ago years. I understood how such a structure could be useful as a church, as it likely held some sort of larger space used for meetings.

And so it proved. Inside the front door, we were directed forward by a couple of ushers, middle-aged men in ragged clothes and pleasant expressions. Passing out of the small atrium, we entered a larger meeting room, with a stage constructed at the far end. Ranged before it were rows of folding chairs, all rather new, and likely paid for by our client by way of his daughter. We found seats together close to the front on the right side. The room was nearly full, and there were a number of low conversations, but by some mutual consent, none of them ever became loud or jolly – just an even hum that never ceased. There were always constant glances toward the stage, where there were three chairs placed in the shadows behind a worn and leaning lectern. On one of these, sitting slumped in seeming weariness with his gaze directed downward upon a Bible held in his hands, was Reverend Philo Tate Simmons, apparently in deep contemplation.

This continued for a moment or two until a tall well-dressed woman appeared from somewhere back-stage. She was in her mid-twenties, and carried herself with authority and grace. She glanced around the audience, and I could see when she recognized the man beside us – likely her father – although Holmes and I apparently caused no interest – just more faces in the crowd. She did not seem surprised to see him there, but she also gave no sign of acknowledgement. As she leaned down to whisper into Simmons' ear, the room fell silent, as if this was a sign that they recognized, and the only sound that was immediate to Holmes and me was Hellifield's somewhat stertorous breathing and the rustle of his clothes as he nudged Holmes to indicate that the young woman was his daughter, Lydia.

Meanwhile, on the stage Simmons was rising while Lydia Hellifield sat down in the chair that he had vacated, leaving the other two empty. Simmons had taken a couple of steps forward and paused, between his seat and the lectern, as if seeking strength to share his message for the evening.

Having seen something of the fire-and-brimstone ministers who preached a form of the Gospel in which only they could be certain to truly avoid eternal Hellfire, I expected Simmons to open his performance with a crazed and foamy diatribe about sin and punishment and exclusion of those who didn't meet the levels of Godly requirement he'd constructed in his own head. I should have known better. This was the man who had provided water to the thirsty in the hottest part of summer, and opened a location to do the work of feeding and healing in one of the city's worst quarters. When he began to speak, I quickly forgot his curious Appalachian accent, so rarely heard here in London, and listened to his actual words.

He began with a quiet welcome, and a reminder that his message would be short, and food would be available after – "Unless someone needs that now more than you need to hear me," he added. A number of people laughed slightly – a sound that I can attest is not heard very often in Whitechapel – but no one felt prompted to rise and seek sustenance.

"Tonight I've chosen Hebrews 13:6," began Simmons. "'Do not neglect to do good and to share what you have, for such sacrifices are pleasing to God.'" He didn't bother to open and read from the Bible in his hand, but I was certain that should I bother to verify later, I'd find that he had quoted correctly. "You might not feel that you have anything to share," continued the speaker, "but God wasn't talking about sharing the coin from your pocket. It's just a piece of metal – man's construct to trade for a share of someone else's time or goods. It only means anything between us because we agree that it does – you and the baker agree that a coin can be traded for the loaf of bread that he baked with his own time, using the flour that he obtained from another man by trading another coin to him for what he had to sell. Remember, Jesus said, 'Render unto Caesar the things that are Caesar's, and unto God the things that are God's. The coin is Caesar's – and it represents what all of has to use to survive on this plane of existence. Some aren't as Christ-like in how they do it – they hoard their coin, or use it to deprive or speculate or overcharge and gouge others, taking more than they can ever use in a dozen lifetimes. We have to be part of such a system – we have no choice, trading our time and the sweat of our brows for food and shelter and a few moments of peace – but we can do so with Christ in our heart, taking no more than we need and finding a way to help those around us whenever possible."

There were nods of agreement around the room, and I found a way to glance at Hellifield beside us. Nothing in Simmons' sermon was specifically addressed toward him, but how could he not feel the tight pinch of some of the words about those who hoard and deprive? Even if he wasn't that way himself – and I didn't know enough about him one way or the other to speculate – he was certainly surrounded by such greed and constant conniving every day in the form of friends and associates. Such talk from a simple minister – con-man or not – was bound to be unpleasant. Nay, it could sound nothing less than dangerous and radical.

Behind the lectern, Simmons already seemed to be finishing his message, announcing for those who were new how the rear of the building could be accessed for the purpose of dining. There was a restless shuffle as people began to gather themselves preparatory to standing when Hellifield suddenly popped up beside us.

"When do you heal people?" he cried, his tone strident and confrontational. He half-raised his cane. On the stage, his daughter rose suddenly, a look of shock and embarrassment crossing her features. Hellifield was indifferent, stepping out into the narrow aisle that ran along the right of the building and awkwardly shuffling forward toward the stage. "My hip has been my cross to bear for half my life," he said. "I ache in places all the time, and other places have been numb for years. I've heard the stories about what you can do, and surely you've heard of me – you were willing enough to take my money to set up this church. Couldn't you have at least offered to use your gifts upon me in return?" He reached the end of the chairs and turned toward the short set of steps leading upward to the stage. "You never even thanked me!"

He paused once while climbing, and then reaching the stage, he began to walk toward Simmons, who towered over the smaller man. Around us people were leaning forward, and a low buzz of conversation filled the room – decidedly more urgent than what we'd heard before the service began.

On stage, Lydia Hellifield took a step forward, reaching for her father. She took his free hand in both of hers, attempting to pull him aside, but the small man gave a little cry, yanked free, and placed himself before the minister.

"Heal me," he demanded.

Simmons looked flustered. He glanced back and forth from daughter to father, appearing to have quickly lost the easy confidence he manifested when speaking to the attentive audience. Finally, coming to some sort of decision, he handed his Bible to Lydia and stepped forward, placing a hand on each of Hellifield's shoulders and leaning down, appearing to whisper in the other man's ear.

Lydia stepped back, and I took a second to glance at Holmes. He was at his most alert, watching what was happening with an unblinking gaze. His lips were tight and his nostrils flared, as if he needed extra air to encourage the hot combustion of his observational skills. I only thought to look back toward the stage when I heard Hellifield give a small cry, similar to that when he'd pulled from of his daughter's grip a moment before.

I was afraid that I had missed something – some flash of power, or indication that the miracle had occurred. I recalled once that I was so intent on watching an eclipse through a specially constructed box (so as to save my eyesight) that I completely missed the rippled shadow bands that seemed to wriggle across the ground during the moments immediately preceding totality. I was regretting that I wouldn't have seen the moment that Hellifield was healed – and clearly I was prepared to believe that he would be – when I was suddenly surprised (along with everyone else in the room, save perhaps Holmes) as the cantankerous man dropped heavily to the ground, as if the minister had turned loose of a large bag of potatoes.

My first thought, no more than a flash across my mind, was that the process had exhausted the older man. But possibly it was the sudden surprise and dismay that flashed across Simmons' countenance that alerted my medical instincts that something was amiss. I rose and was on the stage before I realized that had occurred. But it took no great medical skills to see that Hellifield was dead.

The look on his face was abominable. His colour was pale, there was foam around his mouth, tinged with blood where he'd bitten through his tongue. As I stood, I became aware that Holmes was beside me. He quickly dropped and examined the body before rising again and turning to the crowd.

"There has been an accident," he said, his commanding tone somewhat silencing the chatter. "Can someone fetch a constable?"

One of the men standing at the rear who had earlier acted as a smiling usher nodded and dashed out. I looked back toward Simmons, who seemed to have shrunk inside his clothing. He was wringing his hands as he shuffled backwards, dropping heavily into one of the three chairs.

Speaking to Lydia Hellifield, still clutching the Bible, Holmes identified us. "I am Sherlock Holmes, and this is Dr. Watson." Although still wearing shabby clothes, he now looked remarkably like himself – standing straighter, his hair combed straight back with his fingers. "Your father asked us here tonight – and he said he had something planned to investigate Pastor Simmons' supposed healing powers." He glanced toward the body at our feet "I gather that he intended to put the minister to the test."

The young woman nodded and swallowed, attempting to speak. Then, "Yes. He's – he had threatened to do something like this, but I never thought it would amount to anything. When I saw him here tonight – I'm involved with several charities, and father is always – was always cynical about each of them equally. He's never tried anything like this before."

"He had suspicions that you and Mr. Simmons might be romantically involved," I explained.

She laughed – an unexpected burst that felt highly inappropriate so near her father's corpse. "What?" She looked toward the man seated nearby, who himself was suddenly looking back at her in surprise. "Him? Impossible."

Simmons stood then, looking possibly more broken than he had just a moment before. "Lydia – " he began, his unusual accent taking on an unpleasant whining aspect, but he was interrupted by the sound of footsteps arriving at the back of the church. I saw that it was a constable, accompanied by our old friend Sergeant Corby. He recognized us immediately but glanced right and left to completely assess the situation before making his way toward the stage.

I glanced back at Holmes to judge his reaction at Corby's arrival, but he was focused intently on Simmons and Lydia Hellifield. Even when Corby arrived and spoke to him, he didn't turn away from them.

After greeting the sergeant, Holmes said, "Mr. Simmons, I believe you were about to speak."

The minister's initial shock at Lydia Hellifield's statement was now more controlled. Clearly he had been rocked back by the raw contempt she had conveyed toward him in just three short words. He shook his head, but Holmes pressed him.

"I believe that you were surprised that your feelings for Miss Hellifield were not reciprocated as you had believed. The expression on your face could have no other interpretation."

Simmons nodded and licked his lips. His fingers twitched, as if he wanted something to grasp – his Bible, perhaps, still in the young lady's hands, or possibly her throat.

"I thought we had an understanding," he said softly, his curious American accent giving his puzzlement an aspect of pathos. "We found this church building together. She believed in me – in the work we were doing. We had plans – a future." He looked toward the woman. "Lydia... ?" His voice trailed off.

Lydia Hellifield showed no hesitation, however, in conveying her thoughts. "A future?" The contempt in her voice was palpable. I heard a rustling behind me and realized that the congregation – momentarily forgotten – was still there, as if they were paying customers watching a play in which I was suddenly now one of the actors. I turned to look out at them. Everyone was still and quiet, and oblivious as several more constables quietly entered and placed themselves at the doors and up and down the rude aisles.

Philo Tate Simmons seemed to be collapsing in upon himself – a set of clothes that was emptying as we watched while the poor figure in them evaporated. Never have a seen a man emotionally crushed so quickly. He seemed to age in front of our eyes, sagging to a stoop and suddenly taking on an ashen tone to his skin.

With a sneer, Lydia Hellifield made as if to step toward him, raising the Bible in order to return it to him.

"Stop!" cried Holmes, surprising us all. "Why don't you keep that Bible for just another moment, Miss Hellifield." He said it with certainty, and she seemed to have no choice but to respond.

Glancing quickly toward me before returning his gaze to the young lady, Holmes asked, "How did he die?"

I turned toward the body. "One might initially think it was a fit of some sort – an apoplectic seizure of terrible strength." Holmes seemed to be waiting for more, and I obliged. "But he also shows every indication of receiving a massive, concentrated, and fast-acting dose of cyanide. But," I added, "there is no smell of it on his breath."

"Injected," was Holmes's reply. "Sergeant," he said, continuing to watch the girl intensely. "Would you and one of the constables stand on either side of this lady? But not too close!" he added quickly.

"Now, Miss Hellifield," he continued to the young woman, who watched him the way that a small mammal becomes frozen before a cobra. "Open the Bible."

There was no movement on her part. She continued to stare at Holmes, who took a step to one side, so that he was beside her father's body. Her eyes followed him, and did so again when he knelt beside the dead man.

"Your father asked us to see about debunking Mr. Simmons' abilities to heal by faith," said Holmes. "He visited us this morning, and I spent the afternoon researching the minister's background in the United States. I found nothing to indicate any falsity. But I didn't just spend my time examining that piece of the puzzle. I asked questions about you and your father as well."

At that point he gestured to the corpse, and the woman, hypnotized by his every word, involuntarily looked down. She seemed to see the dead man for the first time, and she gave a small shudder, as if understanding the reality of it all. Her tightly pressed fingers were white on the Bible.

Holmes stood. "Your relationship with you father has always been contentious – it's a well-known fact, and more-so since the death of your mother. And while he has left you on a long leash, you've been tied to him far more than you wished. That is no secret, either. Your constant demands for financial freedom and your 'fair share' of his fortune has been quite the talk of your social set. Fortunately I know a fellow who sits in a web and feels the vibrations of this sort along every strand, and he was able to give me a very sharp description of you – and what you might be capable of – and the fact that you are your father's only heir, and during recent arguments, he has threatened to disinherit you.

Holmes took a step toward Lydia Hellifield, bracketed as she was on both sides by the sergeant and constable. "You weren't surprised to see your father in the audience tonight. I suspect that he bragged or hinted about some plan of his to come here and test Mr. Simmons' abilities – to demand a healing of his afflictions, as we saw. So you came prepared as well." Once again he commanded, "Open the Bible."

Lydia Hellifield apparently realized that she had no alternative, or perhaps Holmes's tone was such that she was unable to do other than as he demanded. She held out her hands and let the book split open, revealing a shiny glass object, thin and long, pushed into the gutter between pages. I recognized it at once as a hypodermic needle, with a long thin needle and still partly full of some clear liquid.

"Hellifield said he had numbness over parts of his body – the location of these parts you would know," continued Holmes. "He possibly didn't even feel when you stepped up to him as he climbed on stage, taking his hand and pushing in the needle, using the plunger to inject him with a massive dose of cyanide. By the time he was standing before Mr. Simmons, it was too late – he was seconds from death.

"I try to observe everything," added Holmes. "It would have been natural to keep one's eyes on the main drama – the minister and the sick man. But I watched you as well. You reached out for your father, he grimaced and pulled away – certainly that was when you killed him – and then you stepped back, slipping something that glinted for the shortest second into the Bible handed to you by Mr. Simmons. Even as I approached the stage after your father's sudden death, I never took my eyes off of you. I'll testify that you were the one who slipped something into the Bible – the hypodermic – and that Mr. Simmons only touched your father for the briefest of instants on both shoulders. I have no doubt that an autopsy will show that a hypodermic needle entered your father by way of his arm – the same arm that you grasped when he came up here."

And so it proved, but the examination of the corpse didn't occur until the next day. That night at Simmons' church, Holmes reached and gently took the Bible and its damning evidence while a mute Lydia Hellifield was led away by Sergeant Corby – who only had the vaguest sense of what had happened, but knew from his past associations with Holmes that an iron-clad case existed, nonetheless.

Simmons was bereft. I accompanied him to his bleak little room in a squalid house in Tilley Street, and several members of his congregation followed, anxious to minister unto him following the terrible shock he'd just endured. I understand that afterwards he never returned to the church, not even once, and soon after departed England entirely. I have no knowledge of his whereabouts, and if he does continues to minister, it is in such a way that has attracted no attention.

Later that night I returned to Baker Street to find Holmes smoking his pipe by the fireplace, cheery flames seeming to deny both the events of the night and the cooling October weather. I informed him that Simmons was being cared for, but the poor fellow seemed shattered.

"We may never know how things turn out," said Holmes. "We've intersected with these people for just a few hours – just enough to understand what happened tonight – but with no true knowledge of the overall picture."

"Such as," I added, "whether Simmons can really perform miracles."

Holmes nodded. "Events made that question irrelevant. And Hellifield tried to force an answer before I'd even had a chance to conduct a true investigation – typical of such impatient men."

"One might even be tempted to say that he accelerated his own death," I said. "Hiring you likely gave him the idea to go ahead and confront Simmons at the church, demanding to be healed. It's probable that his daughter had some inkling of what he intended to do, as you speculated, and decided to move forward with her own plan of killing him herself, and then framing the minister by putting the syringe into his Bible. But surely," I continued, a thought popping into my head, "she could have simply hoped that her father's death would be put down to a fit, with no autopsy performed. Why reveal the syringe at all by leaving it to be found in the Bible, which would be returned to Simmons. He would certainly discover it almost immediately, and more importantly, would know who had put it there, and what that implied."

"I suspect that her motivations were complex, but perhaps she wanted Simmons to know what she had done for some reason. Possibly she wasn't quite finished with him yet, and that tie, no reinforced with a secret between them, would be of some use. Or she could have intended Simmons to be murdered quite soon too, and wasn't worried about what he did or did not know. She may have just wanted a place to hide the syringe that wasn't on her person, and it was easiest to frame the minister by handing it over to him in the Bible as soon as possible. The ways of women," he summarized, taking a draw on his pipe, "are inscrutable. How can one come to any conclusions when attempting to build on such quicksand?"

A month or so later, I happened to pass through Whitechapel and took an impulsive turn into Lincoln Street. In most directions were poverty and death, and the public house was still doing a rousing business. But I was happy to see that in some small way, the church was continuing its mission, despite its loss of both minister and easy funding, open as something of a soup kitchen and doss house for the neighbourhood's unfortunates. Remembering the gentle words of Pastor Simmons, wherever he might be, and even those of Thaddeus Hellifield when discussing the poor, I climbed the steps to see if they needed any help.

EPILOGUE

VV341

VV341.

A clue left in a room,

A card next to the gun,

And Porlock a *nom de plume*.

VV341.

A body on the floor

Where the dire deed was done.

Too many clues left, for sure.

VV341.

Clothes in a bundle wrapped.

A man kept from the sun,

Like a rat in a wainscot trapped.

VV341.

A dumb bell in the moat.

Holmes had him on the run

And fished out his overcoat.

VV341.

Holmes was right, we perceive.

Now is his tale begun,

A catalogue of intrigue.

VV341.

Vermissa Valley Town.

Friendship kept by a gun,

Whose bullets will cut you down.

VV341.

Goodwill and charity

Were second here to none,

Save the murder of the free.

341 The Lodge,

Sworn to kill and enslave.

The bloodhounds leap and dodge

And drag him to the grave.

VV341.

Lost overboard at night.

A masterstroke from one

Whose lean face grins with delight.

VV341.

A touch – a distinct touch

Of the All Evil One

And his labyrinthine clutch.

Kelvin I. Jones.

www.ingramcontent.com/pod-product-compliance
Lightning Source LLC
Chambersburg PA
CBHW080743250626
47162CB00010B/3007